## "I'll sit on the bed and rub your neck."

As Maria began the massage, Brand said, "Mmm, that's better, but you mustn't get cold...."

"I won't. You—" She stopped. She could feel his warmth, his strong and powerful neck. *Leave now,* her mind told her. Something was happening to them; an electric tension was building. Her hand faltered as he touched her face. Then he pulled her to him and kissed her.

"I'd better go," she said, scarcely able to breathe for the pounding of her heart.

"You haven't finished my neck yet," Brand murmured as he pulled aside the covers. "Lie here where it's warm while you finish."

Maria knew that she shouldn't. She knew also that she was going to.

# MARY WIBBERLEY

## devil's causeway

# *Harlequin Books*

TORONTO • LONDON • LOS ANGELES • AMSTERDAM
SYDNEY • HAMBURG • PARIS • STOCKHOLM • ATHENS • TOKYO

Harlequin Presents edition published February 1982
ISBN 0-373-10486-3

Original hardcover edition published in 1981
by Mills & Boon Limited

# CHAPTER ONE

MARIA stood on the edge of the land and looked out towards the island that wasn't an island. At low tide the causeway—the Devil's Causeway—appeared. Even now the raging sea was receding, reluctantly, from the wide pathway. The wind whipped her long dark hair about her face, and she snuggled deeper into her thick sheepskin coat, hands tight in pockets, breathing deeply of the salt-laden air and tasting the salt on her lips. There were tears in her eyes as she looked towards the island. She couldn't see the house from where she was, only mist outlined trees and rocks. It was a desolate place, miles away from anywhere, out of sight of the world. A place for lovers to be alone, safe from everyone, secure with each other. Only no more, no more. Her father, the man she loved most in the world, driving away with his lover Isobel, had been killed instantly, as had she.

Maria tasted her tears, mingling with the salt spray. She hadn't wanted to come, but it had to be done. She had to go to the house and remove all traces of personal items, collected over a period of fifteen years with love. She closed her eyes, unable to see anything any more, and began to walk towards her car, stumbling slightly over hummocks of dry grass as she went. No more would they come here, on those snatched visits, to be together, to love . . .

She wiped her face with tissues and started the car and began to drive slowly along the bumpy track towards the causeway. Gulls wheeled around the car, and the rain lashed the windscreen mercilessly, obscuring it within seconds, the windscreen wipers fighting a losing battle to keep it clear. Maria drove carefully, slowly, and the half mile seemed to take forever.

Then she was on the island, and could see the narrow pitted track ahead. Trees grew in profusion, tough, bent by the winds, clinging for life to the rocky ground. No one in their right mind could ever imagine this as a love-nest, an idyllic place—which was why no one, in all these years, had ever known the truth. Only Maria.

Then she saw, ahead of her, the house. There was an ache inside her, a deep pain of anguish. She knew then, in that moment, why they had chosen it. It was small, stone-built, very solid-looking, with trees round it almost as if protectively. There was no garden, just the house, with higher ground behind it, surrounded by bushes and long grass. The rain lashed down on the slate roof, and the door was firmly closed—and yet as if waiting for her to come. There was an air of waiting stillness about the place. She shivered, suddenly cold. Climbing out, she slammed the door before the wind could whip it from her and ran across the muddy path, key in hand, towards that door.

She realised that there shouldn't have been smoke coming from the chimney at the same moment that the door was flung open as she fumbled to open it.

She gasped, shocked, disbelieving, and raised her head to see the man standing in front of her, looking at her with an equally shocked look on his face.

Then he spoke. As she stumbled in, and he stepped back to let her, he said: 'Who are you?'

She pushed the hair out of her eyes, the better to see him, and she had to look up to do so. He was a very tall, big man, powerful, strong-looking, with dark hair and dark cold eyes that were looking at her with hostility. All that much Maria could take in in the few moments he gave her before repeating his question, this time more impatiently.

She found her voice. 'Never mind who I am,' she retorted. 'Who are *you*? You have no right to be here!'

'Haven't I?' His glance took her all in. 'How the hell do you know that?'

'Because this house belongs to——' she stopped. She had no intention of telling anything to a perfect stranger. It was a frightening situation, potentially dangerous. He could be an escaped prisoner—no, he couldn't be that, he looked too tidy, his clothes were too expensive—she didn't understand anything, except that she was alone. Why, oh, why hadn't she let Tony come with her? For the first time she regretted the refusal of his offer.

'Yes? To whom?' he asked, and he intended getting an answer.

She shook her head. 'I—must have come to the wrong place. I'm sorry. Is there another house on this—island?'

There seemed to be a long pause before he answered. Then: 'No. This is the only one.'

'And is it called Rhu-na-Bidh?' She waited, breathless, for the answer.

'It is. So—you're here, I'm here—both of us thinking we have the right.' He half turned away and looked towards the fireplace wherein a large fire crackled and glowed. Then he looked back at her. The look was a hard, shrewd, assessing one. He had veiled the hostility for the moment, but it made him no less intimidating. He looked to be the kind of man who was used to getting exactly what he wanted. 'Perhaps we'd better talk.'

A dangerous man, but perhaps, for the moment, going to be polite. He added: 'I'll make you a hot drink. You look as though you need one. Tea or coffee?'

'Tea, please.'

'Better take your coat off—until you go.'

Maria scarcely noticed the significance of the last three words, so busy was she turning over the possibilities in her mind. A squatter? That could be the only explanation. No one in the world knew of the existence of the house. Only three people ever had, and of those three, Maria was the only one still living. Her father would not have wanted her to be in any danger. He would expect her to leave ——

'Put it on the chair near the fire,' his words interrupted her thoughts, and she obeyed, watching him walk out of the room and into the kitchen.

The chair by the fire was an old comfortable-looking rocker. She spread her coat over its back and stood to warm her frozen hands by the blazing fire. The sweater and trousers that she wore were warm, but she still felt chilled with the shock. She couldn't stay, that was obvious, but after that, she didn't know what she would do. Return with the police? Impractical. The nearest village was ten miles away, and she wasn't even sure it had a police station. And she had to go soon. The causeway remained uncovered for only an hour or so in every twelve. She must go . . .

The man returned carrying a beaker and handed it to her. 'Sugar?'

She shook her head. 'No, thanks. Thank you.' The tea was strong and hot.

'Sit down,' he said, 'warm yourself.'

She could hardly refuse. It might be better to humour him. She sat down on a buffet stool, and he remained standing, looking down at her.

'All right,' he said, 'I think you'd better tell me who you are.'

'My name's Maria Fulford——' She looked up at the sudden, shocked sound of his sharply indrawn breath and saw his face change, darken. She was frightened, very frightened at the anger she saw, and she stood up and moved away.

'You—*you* are *his* daughter?' He almost spat the words. Dizzily, feeling as if she were standing on shifting sands, Maria could only stare at him. She couldn't speak. This was a nightmare. What was happening?

'Do you want to know who I am?' he said, voice relentless. She nodded.

'My name is Brand Cordell. I am Isobel's son.'

She thought she was going to faint. For a moment the room seemed to tilt out of balance, and she put her beaker on the table. Her father had never told her of this . . . Dear God, he was Isobel's *son*. This man, this hostile stranger that she had mistaken for a squatter was the son of the woman her father had loved for fifteen years. And, judging by the look on his face, he had known nothing of the affair—until recently. How recently, she was about to find out. At that moment she was incapable of anything, any coherent thought at all.

'You knew all about it, didn't you?' he said harshly.

She found the power to speak. 'Yes,' she whispered.

'Do you know when I found out?' he continued relentlessly. 'I found out just a few hours ago, here.' Numbed, frozen with the shock she still felt, Maria stared at him, white-faced. He picked up a sheaf of papers that had been lying on the table. 'I found letters—and poems.' Contempt filled his voice. 'I found out that my mother had been coming here for years with a married man—had been having an affair with your father!' His eyes blazed anger and she saw his fists clench as he flung the papers from him as though he couldn't bear to touch them; she thought that he was going to strike her, and backed away, physically afraid of him.

It was as if he read her mind. 'I'm not going to *touch* you,' he said. 'Just leave. That's all I ask——' His voice was harsh.

Maria found her strength. Still shaken, but recovering fast, she cut in: 'I've come here for a reason,' she said, 'not to be told to go by *you*.'

'I'm not staying here with you,' he cut in.

'Then why don't *you* go?' she shot back. 'I've travelled up from London today, I'm damned if I'm going to walk out again the minute after I've arrived——'

'There's only one bed,' he said. 'Or did you suppose they had separate bedrooms?'

Her head jerked back with the icy contempt of his words. 'Your mother died three months ago,' she said, as calmly as she could. 'Had you forgotten——'

'I'll never forget.' His eyes were as bleak and hard as flint. 'Nor that your father was responsible——'

He got no further. Incensed beyond reason, Maria reached out and slapped him hard across his face. He gripped hold of her wrist and pulled her towards him. 'Don't you like the truth?' he said bitterly. 'If she hadn't been here with him it would never have happened——'

'But it did!' she gasped. 'Let go of my arm, you're hurting——'

He released her, flinging her arm away as if the touch offended him. 'I despise him,' he said. 'A married man who——'

'You know nothing!' she shouted, rubbing her wrist where he had gripped. His strength frightened her, but she was beyond physical fear now. 'You don't understand——'

'I understand enough,' he cut in. 'I've seen all I want to——'

'What kind of man are you to talk like this?' she demanded. 'They were both adults. Who the hell do you think you are to judge others, tell me *that*!'

'You condone an affair that went on for years?'

'I neither condoned nor disapproved—because it was nothing to do with me!'

'Or your mother? His wife?'

Maria went still. How could she tell him? She took a deep breath. 'My mother is an actress—they lived their own lives——'

'Then why didn't they get divorced?'

She shook her head. She was beginning to feel ill with the terrible tension, the hatred that flowed from this man. 'I don't know——'

'I thought you knew it all,' he said harshly.

Maria went to the rocking chair and sat down before her legs gave way, leaned forward and put her head in her hands. Suddenly she felt herself being pulled to her feet, and she gasped and opened her eyes. 'Tell me,' he said, 'how did you feel when you first found out?'

'I was—shocked,' she admitted, 'but they loved each other very much—don't you see? They loved——'

'Love?' He released her abruptly so that she nearly fell. 'Love?' he repeated the word. 'Excitement, the search for the forbidden—that's all it is. There's no such thing as love.'

'Didn't you love your mother?'

'That's different. Vastly different—but don't try and justify an affair by using that worn-out word!'

'My God, you're bitter!' she exclaimed. 'What's the matter, can't women stand you?' For a moment she thought she thought she had gone too far. For one moment it was as though he was going to strike her. Then he stepped away from her.

'It's a good job you're a woman,' he said slowly.

'I'm sorry, I shouldn't have said that,' she answered.

'But you did.' He sighed, and she saw the lines of pain in his face. Pain—and fatigue. 'Perhaps we've both said things that might be better unsaid.' He ran his hands over his cheeks and forehead. 'What have you come here to do?'

'To remove anything—personal.' She gestured towards the papers on the table.

'I see. Then you'd better get on, hadn't you?' He went over towards the window, and it was as if all aggression had gone—temporarily anyway. The atmosphere was no longer hostile. Some sort of truce had been declared. 'The tide will be in again very soon. We won't be able to leave today now.'

'I—came prepared to stay overnight,' Maria said.

'So did I.' He turned to face her. 'You're safe. I'll sleep down here, you can have the bed upstairs.'

'Thank you.' It was growing dusk outside. 'There's no electricity, is there?'

'No, but I found two oil lamps in the kitchen. I'll get them lit.' He walked out, and Maria watched him go. She was empty of all emotion. Perhaps he was too. Perhaps that was why he was being—civilised, at any rate. No more. Whatever the reason, it was sufficient. She couldn't have taken much more of what had just happened. Brand Cordell was a big, dark, attractive man. She had said what she had in bitter anger and retaliation, but she had known the lie in the words even as she had. He was darkly handsome, strong-featured, dark grey eyes, hawklike profile. She had once seen a photograph of his mother, and she had been beautiful, the similar features softened and gentled by her femininity. No, this man would have many women after him. His bitterness was undoubtedly caused by his so recent shock.

The dancing yellow light softened his features, and as he set the lamp on the table he looked very dark and shadowed. 'I'd better drive your car round the back,' he told her. 'It's more sheltered there, where mine is. Give me your keys.'

Maria opened her bag. 'I've brought food,' she said, 'I didn't think there'd be any here——'

'There is. Tinned and dried stuff, obviously, but enough for days. You'd better take it when you leave tomorrow.'

'Are you going then too?'

He walked towards her, holding his hand out for her keys. 'There's no reason for me to stay,' he answered. 'Is there?'

'No.' As she handed him the keys, their fingers touched, and it was like having an electric shock. 'I'm sorry you had to find out like this,' she said. 'Truly sorry. I'd adjusted, you see. I'd known for a while.'

He stood there very still, just looking down at her face; both were shadowy, and a kind of tension seemed to fill the room, surrounding and filling them, and it was a different kind from what had been before. It was totally different and unexpected, and Maria felt her heart beat faster. She didn't understand it, but something was happening to her, neither unpleasant nor frightening, just—different from anything that had gone before. And Brand Cordell was aware of it equally. He didn't move away, even though he had the keys and he could have gone.

'I've said things I regret,' he said. 'I said them in anger, and a deep hurt.'

'It's all right,' she answered, 'I know.'

Her eyes met his, and she heard his indrawn breath. He seemed very big and powerful, and he was all man, that was certain, a powerful male animal who had, rightly perhaps, felt an intense bitterness towards her.

And Maria, knowing this, did something she had no conscious knowledge of intending to do. She reached up her hand and touched his cheek very gently, the cheek where she had slapped him hard in her own anger and pain.

'I regret striking you,' she said softly. 'Forgive me.'

There was a shimmering instant when time seemed to stand still, a pause in the world, then he had taken her hand and held it gently for a few moments.

'I know,' he answered. There was, briefly, the same sensation there had been when she had passed him the keys, like an electric current flowing between them, only that had been momentary; this was something that went on for ever.

Then he let her hand go, and turned away. 'I'll bring your things in,' he said, as he went towards the door.

Maria remained standing where she was. 'Back seat. One case, one box of food,' she said. The door closed behind him, and Maria discovered that she was shivering. She closed her eyes. What was happening was absurd. She was a sane, level-headed woman of twenty-three, with a devoted fiancé-to-be, Tony, a good job in advertising, and a well-adjusted life-style. So why was she shivering because a man had touched her?

She moved abruptly, to free herself of the ridiculous spell, and turned her coat round, looking into the dancing flames of the fire. They would leave tomorrow, say goodbye, part, and they would never see each other again. And that was as it should be. Only another sixteen hours or so, that was all. She picked up her beaker of tea and carried it into the kitchen. Another oil lamp burned on a dresser, lighting the room with soft glow, and she looked round her, aching with sadness for what had been.

She heard a car's engine and went to the window. Dimly through the growing dusk she saw Brand Cordell getting out, leaning in to lift out case and box, and she found the back door and opened it, and let him in.

It was nearly midnight and she was very tired, drained with the emotion brought about sorting and burning several dozen letters and personal papers that had accumulated over the years. They had let the fire go down, and had been sitting together at the table for hours.

Brand suddenly sat back and rubbed his forehead. 'I'm tired,' he said.

'So am I. I'll make us a drink. What'll it be, tea or coffee?'

'There's a bottle of Scotch in the kitchen. That'll help you sleep better,' he answered. He lifted one eyebrow in question.

'Yes, it would.' Maria dreaded going to bed. She never slept well away from home, and this would be particularly poignant. 'Thanks.'

'There are two glasses as well. We'll drink in style.'

He went out. Two glasses. They would have sat by the fire, at night, having a drink out of those same glasses, talking, the hours slipping past swiftly—she could almost picture them, her father smiling, Isobel responding, loving each other, a love that would never have died, perhaps never would now. They would be together for always.

'I'm sorry.' Brand had come in so quietly that she hadn't seen him standing there with the glass, beside her, so lost had she been in reverie. She took it from him.

He lifted his own glass. 'Cheers,' he said.

'Cheers.' She sipped slowly. She rarely drank, and then never whisky, but it seemed to be what she needed at that moment. The whole situation was bizarre. She was sitting by the glowing embers of a dying fire with a man who had been a perfect stranger only hours previously. He still was, and yet there was a tenuous link stretching out from the past, and it touched them both. It was a link of love, and ultimately, tragedy. Both had lost a parent in the same few minutes. She knew nothing more about him, save his name, and his age, thirty-five. She didn't know if he was married or single, or where he lived, or how. The atmosphere since he had come back in with her luggage had been one of polite truce, there was no other way to describe it. It was as though some part of him were held in tight check.

They had eaten toast and tinned pâté, neither being hungry. They had drunk several cups of coffee, but there had been little conversation. The grim task had been too personal for trivial words, and the emotions roused in Maria too deep to speak about.

Now she was as exhausted as if she hadn't slept for days. She put her hand to her eyes and rubbed them gently. When she looked across at Brand again he was looking at her.

'There are things we have to discuss before we leave tomorrow,' he said.

She felt her heart bump in apprehension. 'About what?' she queried.

He shook his head. 'Not tonight. The morning will do.' He seemed almost grim. She wanted to know, and yet she didn't.

'Then if you're not going to tell me, I'll go up to bed.'

'Of course. There's a kettle of hot water outside. Leave it at the top of the stairs when you've used it, I'll collect it.'

She drained her glass. 'Thanks, I will.'

The toilet was downstairs, in a room beyond the kitchen. It was a fairly primitive affair, leading to a septic tank, and she collected the kettle on her way back in, and up the stairs. Not knowing what bedding, if any, there would be, Maria had brought two sheets and a pillowcase. There was, however, ample, including blankets and a duvet. She had given Brand sufficient, and they had been aired for several hours before the fire. She settled herself down after washing and undressing and lay for a few minutes looking towards the opened uncurtained window. The rain had stopped and cold damp air rolled in, making her feel warmer in contrast.

She heard quiet footsteps on the stairs, the faint metallic rattle of the kettle being moved, and then his footsteps descending. Then there was silence.

She lay awake for what seemed ages, heart full of mixed emotions, brain going over the day's events, until eventually she fell into a light troubled sleep.

When she awoke it was pitch dark outside, and she was starving. She was so hungry that her stomach ached. She remembered that she had eaten very little all day. Knowing that she wouldn't get to sleep again, she slid out of bed, fumbled for her dressing gown and crept down the unfamiliar stairs holding firmly to the banister rail. There was silence from the living room, although the door was open. She wondered if Brand was asleep.

Feeling her way, remembering the loaf she had left on the working top, she found it and took out two slices of bread. Her hand brushed the packet of butter beside it and the knife. The faintest glimmer of light came from the window, now that her eyes were used to the darkness, and she managed to butter one slice of bread, then put the second slice on top. Hardly a luxury meal, but it would be sufficient to assuage the pangs.

Mouth watering, she picked up the bread, about to put it to her mouth ——

Crash! She was knocked violently to the floor, and a crushing weight was on her, stifling her, smothering her—she tried to scream, felt hard hands on her body, then ——

'What the hell——!' The weight was gone, she was pulled to her feet, and she saw the tall dark familiar outline of Brand Cordell in front of her. That was the moment she screamed.

## CHAPTER TWO

THE next moment she was being led into the living room, pushed on to the settee, still dazed and semi-conscious with shock and fear. Light bloomed and Brand moved near to her.

'I thought I'd got a burglar,' he said. 'Are you all right?'

She shook her head. 'Not yet,' she croaked. The crushing weight of his body had literally knocked the breath out of her for a few seconds. She still trembled with shock. Her body felt bruised all over and she wasn't sure what had happened.

He vanished and she heard the clink of metal, the hiss of flaring Calor gas, and she sat by the ashes of the dead fire shivering with the cold. Brand's bedding was on the settee. She pulled the duvet round her and felt warmer. When he came in and handed her a hot beaker she looked up at him. 'I didn't know I'd woken you,' she said. Her voice was coming back.

'Some slight—noise—alerted me. I didn't stop to think—I'd forgotten anyone was here.' He paused. 'I saw a shape, something moving——'

'And that something was me,' she said, less croakily now that the hot coffee had warmed her throat. She saw then that he wore only underpants, and he moved away and put on his trousers as if suddenly aware of his omission. In the brief moments before he did so she saw the build of him, the hard lean muscular body, no spare fat, long legs, built like an athlete. She closed her eyes briefly. When she opened them he was, if not fully dressed, at least respectable.

'There's nothing I can say will make you feel better,' he said. 'Except to apologise if I was rough. I acted instinctively.'

'Yes, I gathered that.' She rubbed her shoulder. 'Now I know how a rugby player feels after being tackled!' She winced at the pain. 'I'd only come down because I was hungry. Heaven knows what happened to my bread and butter.'

'I'll get you some more,' he said, and vanished like a wraith. Considering his size, he moved quickly and quietly. Sensation was returning to her numbed body, and she ached all over. There was something he had said—what was it? She frowned, remembered. 'I'd forgotten anyone was here.' That was it. He had forgotten? After all the traumas, the emotion? He must have been in a very deep sleep. Which made his silent waking all the more remarkable. To wake from deep slumber, to act so instinctively—and silently—that she had no warning of his approach indicated a man of some force and power. Maria had already sensed this about him during the course of the evening. After the bitter recriminations following her arrival, he had seemed to be holding himself in check, controlled, and in a strange way that much more forceful because of it. Maria, sitting sipping her coffee and gradually becoming warmer as moments passed, found her thoughts were crystal clear, and she was wide awake.

The stunning physical attack had had the effect of sharpening her perception remarkably, and in a moment of blinding clarity she realised that she had never met anyone in her life remotely like this man. She did not like him. She could not. Despite their tragic link, he was a stranger, one who had said unforgivable things; who had made her question herself and her reaction to life. He was very disturbing.

'Here, I found some of the cheese I'd bought.' He

handed her a plate with a sandwich on it. He had also brought himself a beaker of coffee. He sat on the rocking chair and she threw a blanket across to him.

'Put that round your shoulders, it's chilly,' she said.

'Thanks. So it is.' The light from the lamp was soft and warm, but the room was still very cold. He wrapped the blanket round him. 'It's nearly four o'clock,' he said. 'After we've finished our drinks we'd better try and get some sleep.'

Maria wasn't sure if she would be able to, but she nodded. She didn't want to be sitting with him, in the enforced intimacy, for longer than necessary. She ate the cheese sandwich as quickly as possible, then stood up. 'I'll finish my coffee in bed,' she told him. She had some aspirins in her bag upstairs, and she was going to take two, but she didn't want to tell him that either. She didn't want him to feel guilty, or responsible for her condition, even though he was. It was as though she wished to keep herself apart from him—and she didn't quite understand her own reaction. She was beginning to feel confused about a lot of things.

He stood up as well. 'Of course,' he answered. They were several feet apart, he with blanket-draped shoulders, she in nightie and dressing gown, and it was four o'clock on a cold autumn morning, and just the two of them in a small remote from anywhere cottage with no other human life for many miles. The sudden realisation of that fact was overwhelming—and apparently mutual—for an instant and devastating tension filled the room. Maria couldn't move. Quite suddenly, she couldn't move away. Pain filled her body, and her mind. She gave a little groan, and her body was stiff.

Brand watched her, but made no attempt to move towards her. It was as if he too was incapable of motion. 'What is it?' he said harshly, and the spell was broken.

'Nothing. I——' The beaker fell on to the carpet and she heard it go and looked at it as if wondering who had done that—and he bent to pick it up. The drops remaining had spilled. With his movement she too was free. She pulled the duvet from where she had dropped that too and put it back on the settee, and turned away, but Brand caught her arm.

'Wait,' he said. She wrenched herself free, gasping, panicking.

'No!'

'For God's sake, woman, what is it? What happened?'

'Nothing. I dropped the beaker, that's all. My hand——' She looked at her fingers. She didn't know why or how, but her fingers were all right, she was just tired. She put her hand to her forehead, and it was burning and she shook with an uncontrollable trembling that filled her.

She stumbled as she turned away, to escape from the intolerable prison of his nearness, and she would have fallen down if his reflexes hadn't been lightning-fast. He held her by the arms, supporting her, and his hands were warm and very strong. Too strong.

'I'm all right,' she said, voice blurred with the sudden exhaustion and fear of something unknown to her.

'Like hell you are,' his voice grated. 'I'll take you up. You could fall down the stairs——'

'No, I won't—I——'

He made an impatient sound, moved, and the next moment he had picked her up in his arms as though she were a child. Carrying her, he walked out of the door into the hallway and up the stairs, slowly, cautiously, and Maria lay in his arms, helpless, feeling the beating of his heart against her body, feeling the hard muscular arms that held her securely, and wanting to weep.

He laid her on the bed and covered her with the blankets, then he felt her forehead. He was sitting on the side of the bed. The room was in darkness, only the faintest echo of the oil lamp reaching into the doorway and outlining it in a pale blur.

'You shouldn't have come here,' he said, but so softly that it was almost as though he spoke to himself. Maria moved her head fretfully to try to push his hand away, and he took it away.

'Go down,' she said. 'I'll sleep now.'

'Your forehead's burning. I'd better get you some aspirins, there are some in the kitchen.'

'There are some in my bag,' she answered, 'if you'll pass it to me. It's on the chair.'

He stood up and handed it to her. 'I'll get you a drop of milk——'

'Water will do——'

'Milk,' he said, as though that settled the argument. 'It's better.'

Maria sat up when he had gone and fumbled in her bag. She nearly dropped the foil packet on the bed, but rescued it, and when he came back in she held the two tablets in her hand. This time he didn't sit down but stood and waited as she swallowed the milk and pills. Something had changed. He was a blank, impersonal stranger again.

She lay back. 'Please go,' she said, and he walked out without a word.

She had nightmares, vague, no memory on waking yet with the lingering aftertaste of fear and sadness with her, and she sat up, still crying after the final one. She ached all over, and it was an effort to actually sit up, and she began to feel frightened. 'Oh God,' she muttered, and climbed painfully out of bed to stand shivering on the carpet. Little men with hammers banged away inside her head, and her whole body felt as if it had been crushed by a steamroller. Painfully, slowly, she put on her dressing gown and went to the head of the stairs. Biting her lip, she began the agonising descent, each step jarring through her. When she reached the bottom and walked into the living room, it was to see a good fire burning, Brand's blankets neatly folded on the settee, and an otherwise empty room. She called his name, but there was no answer, no sound save for the crackling of the coals as they blazed merrily up the chimney. She knew he wasn't in the house, knew it with a certain sure instinct. There was an emptiness there, as of something vital missing.

She walked slowly into the kitchen and looked out of the window. Her Mini and his Land Rover stood in place. The back door was bolted, and both vehicles were empty.

The kettle was full and still warm and she lit the gas to make herself coffee. Careful not to spill or drop anything this time, she filled the beaker, added fresh milk and went to sit by the fire. The room was warm, a great contrast to the middle of the night in more ways than one. She looked around her. He had tidied the papers away, the lamp was in the centre of the table, and her jacket was hanging on a hook near the front door. Outside, a wind blew, but the sun shone, albeit faint and watery, and gulls flew nearby crying their faint harsh cries, wheeling and swooping as though searching for something.

Where was he? He could have gone for a walk, and as it was only ten o'clock he had probably assumed she would still be asleep. It didn't matter. Maria should have been here now on her own anyway, and if she could have turned the clock back she would have done so. Better never to have met him . . .

An hour passed, then two, and she was beginning to feel concerned about his absence. The island wasn't

large, and the only way off it was via the causeway at
low tide, but it wasn't low tide now, that would have
happened much earlier. Suppose he had fallen somewhere? Was hurt? Maria had busied herself in the kitchen, checking cupboards, because although movement was painful, it was even worse when she sat
down. She had just decided that she would have to go
out and search for him when she heard the front door
opening. Her heart leapt in relief, and she went in as
quickly as she could to see him entering. She realised
that this was the first time she had seen him in day-
light. When she had arrived it had been nearly dusk.

He wore a thick, dark blue jacket, jeans, and a dark
blue sweater. He looked like a fisherman, and as
healthy and tanned as one. His face, clearly seen for
the first time, was devastatingly attractive, and her
heart bumped. She had known, she had known, but to
see, now ——

Then he looked across at her. His hair was windswept, thick and dark and untidy, and his wide mouth
was unsmiling. 'Did you wonder where I was?' he
asked.

'Slightly.' She didn't care if he noticed the sarcastic
bite in her word. She felt obscurely angry with him.

He grinned faintly, then brought a box to the table
and put it down. 'I've been shopping,' he said.

'Don't be stupid!' she snapped. 'How could you——'
her voice tailed away. His eyes were narrowed in
amusement. He found her anger *funny*! She wouldn't
give him the satisfaction, so she forced a smile on her
face.

'Well, of *course* you have,' she answered.

He lifted out a bottle of milk, a loaf, and put them
back. 'That's right,' he said. Her smile faded. He
couldn't have been—it was impossible. But he had.

Damn the man! Here she had been, sick with apprehension, aching all over because of his stupid rugby tackle, and he stood there big and smirking—well, almost—because he was enjoying her discomfiture.

'All right,' she said wearily, 'you've enjoyed your little joke. But it seems a bit pointless to me to go shopping when we're leaving soon.' She had no intention of asking him how on earth he'd done it. He'd like that, he was probably waiting for it.

'But we're not. Leaving, I mean,' he answered calmly. 'And before you ask, I went by boat, and bike.'

'Don't be——' She stopped. That was what he wanted her to say. She was seeing a different side of him, and she liked it even less than the other.

He nodded. 'True. You can look out if you want. The bike's at the door, the boat's by the shore. I went out for a walk about eight—found both in an outside shed, realised they were here for the purpose of getting to the mainland when the tide was in, and went. I cycled to the village for food, and for this.' And he lifted out a bottle of liniment. 'For you.'

'What do you mean, we're not leaving?' The words sunk in belatedly.

'Not today. How do you feel?'

'How do you think?' she rejoined dryly.

'Terrible? Which is why I went for the liniment. You're going to ache like hell for a couple of days. There's no possibility of you driving to London in that condition.'

Maria was silenced at last. It was Friday. She had come up deliberately on Thursday so that she could, if necessary, travel back to London slowly with no need for haste, over the weekend. But she didn't like having decisions made for her. On the other hand, her own reason told her that she couldn't, physically, drive as she was now. She sat down.

—'Oh,' she said.

'I've also bought some frozen pizzas for lunch. I'll go and unpack this lot.' He walked out to the kitchen with the box and left her. When he returned he handed her the bottle of liniment. 'I strongly advise you to go and get this on now. The sooner it starts to work, the better.'

She took the bottle. 'I won't offer to help,' he said softly.

Maria stood up. 'Because I'm sure you'd know what the answer would be,' she answered, equally softly, equally sarcastically. She half turned, careful to move as though it didn't hurt her at all—which was difficult. 'You should keep a stock of this in,' she snapped, temper rising fast because of the way he watched her, and unable to help herself. 'I'm sure it would save you journeys if you treat everyone like you treat me!' It was childish, she knew that as soon as the words came out, but too late, they were said.

'It isn't too often that I meet women in circumstances like these,' he rejoined swiftly, and the hard edge in his voice was warning in itself. His eyes were very dark grey, slate grey and harder now. Maria turned, because what he had said could not be answered in any way. She turned and stared at him, the dislike flaring in her eyes, and felt tears spring to them, and blinked furiously. Biting her lip, she looked quickly away before he should see, but too late; she heard his indrawn breath and raw tension filled the room. She wanted to strike him. She hated him.

He moved, and she said: 'Get away from me. Don't touch me!'

'I wasn't going to.' His voice was harsh and deep. 'Do you think I'd want to?'

They were only a foot or so apart, facing each other, the big man, and Maria, tall, slender, aching from too many hurts, some self-inflicted. The room seemed very far away, as if they were alone somewhere from physical reality, as if they stood alone in a different place. 'You are part of something I didn't want to know,' he said. 'Do you think I would willingly touch you?' His eyes were shadowed with anger and pain.

She sensed the tight control of him, and it combined with the tension into an explosive mixture. One word, one look, could trigger off the reaction. There was flashpoint. She was frightened, and she moved instinctively away from him, her heart hammering violently.

'No,' she said. 'No!' Her face was white. She put her hand to her mouth. 'I'm—sorry,' she whispered. The softening would not come from him. She couldn't bear it any longer. Nothing like this had ever happened to her before. She felt the slight relaxing of the tension that her words had achieved, and her heart gradually slowed to its normal beat. 'Do you think it's any easier for me?' she went on. 'You're angry with me because I happened to be the one who turned up yesterday. I can't forget *your* reaction to me, your words—how do you think *I* feel? You frighten me. You—I sense a leashed violence in you—I've had a taste of it, even though accidentally. I don't like this situation any more than you do, and—and I have no defence against you.' She shivered helplessly.

'Defence? Physically, you mean? What kind of man do you think I am?'

'I don't know what kind of man you are. You're a stranger to me. Yes, I suppose I mean physically.'

'You're quite safe,' he cut in, voice harsher. 'I don't hit women, not even those who are capable of getting me angrier than anyone I've ever known.' He clenched his fist. 'And you do—God knows, you do!' His face was bleak. He rammed his clenched fist into the

cupped palm of his other hand. The noise was like a
clap of thunder.

Maria's head jerked back with the sudden shock of
his violent movement. She swallowed hard. Her legs
were trembling like jelly, but she forced herself to
stand still. 'That's what I mean,' she said, in a shaking
voice.

'*That* frightened you? Next time you get me mad
I'll go and chop some wood.' He almost spat the words
out. He was still blazingly angry, but perhaps frac-
tionally less so. Maria choked back the tears that
threatened. She rarely cried, so why now, when she
should control her feelings?

'I'll go up——' She had to get away from him. The
sooner she was better, the sooner she could leave.
Then a thought struck her. It didn't mean *he* had to
stay. 'You don't have to stay here as well. You can go
any——'

'Don't be stupid!' His voice cut into hers like a
knife.

'I can manage. I'm stiff and sore, but I'll live.'

'There's no question now of me going before you
do. It was, after all, as you pointed out, my doing that
you're like this—not that I need reminding. As long as
you don't expect me to apologise every hour on the
hour.'

'Now it's you being stupid!' she snapped. 'Of course
I don't.' It was different. This argument was on a different level; strange how she knew it, but she did. 'It
was an accident, I *know* that. Can't you understand—
I'd rather be alone here anyway? I came alone, I
intended to stay here on my own—it won't be any different.'

'And if you fell—had another accident?'

'Would that bother *you*?'

There was a silence, an awful silence. Then: 'Yes, it

would bother me,' he answered, then he turned and walked away from her and went out through the front door, closing it loudly after him.

The tears came then. Sobbing, nearly blinded by them, Maria made her way up the stairs, into her bedroom, and closed the door after her.

After she had applied the liniment to all the places she could reach, and after she had washed, she changed into her warm sweater and trousers and put some make-up on, which had the desired effect of making her feel better. She had thought well in the past few minutes, and reached certain conclusions. She and Brand were stranded in a way for several more days—possibly not more than two if all went well—but to go on as they were doing would be insupportable. She was going to talk to him, and she would be calm and cool, for it was the only way to be.

Anything else would be impossible. She went down, to find Brand in the living room, sitting at the table with more papers in front of him. He looked up as she entered the room. Before she could change her mind, or even think about what she was doing, she said:

'May I speak to you?'

'Yes. What about?'

She pulled a chair away from the table and sat down. 'We're here for a couple more days at least,' she said. 'I'm sorry for all I've said to you, sorry for losing my temper—please, while we're here, can we be—can we have a truce?'

'I think it better, don't you?' he answered calmly.

'I'm not used to argument. I—I've never been like this before with anyone. I—I rarely lose my temper, although I don't expect you to believe me——'

'I do,' he cut in. 'I'm not usually so aggressive either. In fact——' he paused and looked very steadily at her, 'no one has ever had the effect on me that you have. I've been thinking about it while you were upstairs, and reached pretty much the same conclusions as you just have. We met in—unfortunate—circumstances. Also we're——' He ran his fingers through his hair.

Maria knew he knew what he wanted to say, but didn't know how to. Quietly, she said it for him. 'Whatever circumstances we met under it would be the same, wouldn't it? Is that what you're finding difficult to say?'

His eyes were hard. 'Something like that.'

'There are people who strike sparks off each other. Instant antagonism—for no apparent reason.'

'Yes. Just as there are others who meet and are instantly attracted. I'm not talking particularly about the male-female relationship. It can happen with friends. They meet, they feel as though they've known each other for ever. Yes, that happens.'

'Only with us, it's different,' she said quietly. 'I know that.'

'Yes, it's different.' He put his hands on the table. They were very strong hands, like him. Powerful hands. He was a powerful man, not only physically but mentally. 'We have to accept that we don't like each other, and that we never will. It's not even anything personal. You're an attractive woman, I'm sure you know. It's quite simply something to do with our mental—our inner make-up. We've clashed, pretty violently, almost from the first moment we met—and we'll continue to do so.'

'Therefore, while we're here——' she paused now, waiting.

He nodded. 'We'll behave—we'll *try* to behave in a civilised manner. We'll remember our manners, and treat each other with the courtesy we would afford to perfect strangers who meet briefly.'

Maria sighed. He had summed it up as she had expected, had wanted him to do. 'Yes,' she said quietly. 'I'm sorry about that too. Sorry that it's happened this way.' She looked across the table at him, her clear hazel eyes meeting his darker ones for the first time with perfect honesty. 'Thank you.'

He took a deep breath. 'How do you feel—physically, I mean—now that you've used the liniment?' It was the start of the civilised behaviour.

'Better. It smells a little, doesn't it?' She wrinkled her nose, and Brand smiled, he actually smiled. He had good teeth, and the smile almost reached his eyes.

'I wasn't going to mention it, but—yes, it does.' He stood up.

'We can go in two days, and that's a promise. I *will* be all right by Sunday,' she said.

'I think you will. You've a very positive outlook on life, haven't you?'

'Yes. But is that allowed?'

He frowned slightly. 'Allowed? Sorry, I don't get you.'

It was Maria's turn to smile. 'Just a small attempt at humour. If we're to "get on" in a civilised manner, should we keep away from anything remotely personal?'

'Ah, I see. Yes, of course. And that was? Too personal, I mean?'

'Well, almost.'

Brand nodded, bowed slightly. 'Then I apologise.' He pushed his chair in. 'I put the pizzas on while you were upstairs. They should be nearly ready.'

'We'll eat in the kitchen, shall we?'

'No, here by the fire. You need to keep warm.'

'Of course.' Maria watched him go, reflecting on their conversation. They had clearly both been thinking on the same lines. The new style was a strain—but hardly as great as what had been before. He had said what she had known inside and might not have had the courage to say. 'We don't like each other and never will.' Harsh, blunt words, but said with truth, and calmly, and therefore all the more devastating. And then he had added what she had also known. 'It's quite simply something to do with our mental—our inner make-up.' He had put his finger on it straight away. She had not underestimated his character or strength. She did not like him, but she could respect his mind.

She heard the clatter of plates, a muttered oath, and smiled to herself. The air was cleared. She felt much better already. She would have been ill if things had carried on as they had started. She caught a glimpse of herself in the mirror over the fireplace, tilted at an angle, she could see herself sitting at the table, and saw herself through Brand's eyes for a second or two. He had said that she was an attractive woman, and she knew it to be true, not with any vain conceit, but as a fact of life. She wasn't beautiful, but her face had a glow that came from within.

What she couldn't realise was something that no mirror could tell her. That that day she looked fragile, vulnerable, and because of it, extra feminine. She had a rounded face, with high cheekbones softly accentuated, and because of her tiredness her eyes were faintly shadowed, her mouth was more gentle. She looked away, and watched Brand come in with two plates.

'Sit by the fire on the settee. No trays, I'm sorry. You'll have to balance the plate on your lap. Can you manage?'

'Yes, of course.' She obeyed, and he handed her a plate, and knife and fork. 'Thanks. I'll make coffee afterwards. I feel much better already.'

'Because of the liniment, or our talk?' He sat in the rocking chair and watched her.

'A little of both. I've never had to admit I disliked anyone before, and it's not easy—but here, now, it's become so.'

'Only because we were tearing each other apart. Anything must be better than that.'

'Yes.' She bent her head to her plate, suddenly unable to meet his eyes any more. 'I'm—very hungry.'

'Didn't you have any breakfast?'

'No. I forgot.'

'Forgot?' He sounded amused. 'Do you often forget to eat—ah, no, sorry, cancel that question. Too personal.'

She could laugh then. 'Perhaps we ought to cancel that *rule*. It could lead to constant apology on both sides. No, I don't forget meals—I was just rather concerned about——' She stopped.

'About what?'

'Er——' She concentrated on cutting a bite-sized piece of pizza. 'You'd sort of vanished, and I thought you'd got lost.'

He knew then why she had hesitated. Swiftly he said: 'I would have left a note, but when I set out for a walk I only intended to be away half an hour. Then I saw boat and bike—and the rest you know.'

'Of course.' She could look up now. Perhaps this new behaviour wasn't going to be all that easy after all. 'Quite a bike ride really. No wonder you were gone so long.'

'It wasn't so bad. I've not even been on a bike for years, and that one is a real trusty old sit-up-and-beg. I felt like a village postman cycling into the town.'

It was almost funny, and quite, quite, normal; she could smile genuinely at that remark. 'I suppose so.'

They stopped talking to eat then, and when both plates were empty Maria took them out and filled the kettle. She waited in the kitchen while it boiled. That was another thing—she could go and read in her room. There were several paperbacks in the living room, and she could say she wanted to rest. The less time they spent in each other's company the easier it would be all round, as she knew Brand would appreciate.

Two days would pass very quickly, and she intended to do exercises, again in the privacy of the bedroom, to get back to normal sooner. It wasn't going to be so awful after all. He had a certain sensitivity, that was obvious. He would keep his side of their strange bargain, as she intended to do. And after Sunday, when they drove away, their paths would never cross. She need never see Brand Cordell again. Never.

She looked out of the window, and there was a dry ache in her throat. It had come suddenly, and she didn't understand it at all.

# CHAPTER THREE

MARIA emerged from her bedroom after dusk. She had gone up, ostensibly for a rest, but really to read and exercise. After an hour or two she had fallen into a deep sleep, and when she woke up the room was shadowed. Feeling guilty, she went slowly down the stairs, to find Brand reading a book by the light of the lamp.

He looked up and closed the book. 'Did you have a good rest?'

'Yes, thanks. I read for a while, then went out like a light. I feel fine.'

'Muscles okay?'

'Mmm. Shall I get some food ready?'

'No, it's all prepared. Waiting for you to emerge from slumber.' He stood up. 'I'll fetch it in. Nothing exotic, I'm afraid. Chicken fricassée—tinned, alas.'

'Sounds fine. Want any assistance?'

'No. Your job's making coffee afterwards. It's known as division of labour.' He went out before she could answer, although there was nothing she could say anyway. His manner was bland, polite—strictly neutral. Maria clenched her hands tightly together. It's the best way to be, she thought, of course it is. Her knuckles were white with tension and she wanted to scream. She pressed her hand to her mouth as if to stifle it, and Brand came in and saw her.

'Something the matter?'

She took her hand away quickly. 'No. Just a twinge of pain,' she lied. The lie came too easily, for how could she tell him the truth? She didn't know it

36

herself. 'It's gone now.'

'Okay. Eat this. It doesn't look very exciting, but according to the label on the tin it should taste marvellous.'

It was Friday evening, and what would she be doing if she were in London? Going out with Tony, dining, going on to a club with friends. What did Brand do on Friday evenings? Stay at home with his wife—and family? Or was he a man about town? She looked at him. She wanted to know. No, of course he wouldn't be married. He'd said he didn't believe in love—he could be divorced. That would explain his bitterness.

'Are you married?' the question was out even before she realised, and she heard herself say the words; they seemed to echo in the room and she was filled with horror.

'No, I'm not. I'm not even engaged. Are you?'

'No. I'm sorry, I shouldn't have asked.'

'Oh, I don't mind. Perhaps we should be allowed a couple of personal questions a day. You're not married, or not engaged?'

'Neither.'

'But you do have a boy-friend, I imagine.'

'Yes.'

'Do you love him?'

Maria took a deep breath. It was her own fault. She had started it, so she could hardly refuse to answer him. 'I don't know,' she answered.

Brand ate some chicken before speaking again. 'But you do believe in it?'

'Yes, of course I——'

'But you don't love *him*?'

'I'm sorry, I don't think we should continue with this,' she said.

'Do you find the questions offensive? Or is it that

they're too personal?' He asked it in perfectly calm, almost impersonal tones.

'Not exactly. I just think they're—not important.' Heavens, what was the matter with her? She couldn't even say what she meant.

'Conversation doesn't always have to be about important topics.'

'I know. But we're not——' she stopped. She shook her head, then took a deep breath. 'I just prefer not to continue on this subject, that's all.'

Brand shrugged, 'Fair enough,' and he began eating again. Maria could scarcely do so. Her mouth and throat were dry and she couldn't swallow. She pushed her plate aside. 'I've had enough. I'll go and make us some coffee.' He looked at her half full plate but said nothing.

She stood in the kitchen. She didn't want to know if he was married, so why had she asked? She didn't know that either. She gazed blankly at the kettle. Yet she had. Brand intrigued her in a way no one else ever had. She could only see him in the setting of this cottage, not in London or anywhere else. He had that assured air about him that spoke of success, and money, yet that morning he had cycled on a battered old cycle to the nearest village, and somehow she could see him in her mind's eye doing that with equal aplomb. A strange, complex man. She knew only that his mother had loved her father, nothing else about him, save his name, Branden—shortened to Brand—Cordell, and his age. The Land Rover he drove was a new one. He might live in the country near London. He might possess several cars, and had chosen this one as being practical for remote Scottish roads. He might be a business man, a farmer—anything at all. She didn't like him, and she shouldn't be curious, but she was, intensely so.

The kettle boiled and she switched off the gas. Her hand slipped as she filled the beakers and scalding water gushed hissing over the stove and working top. She jumped back quickly, watching the steaming water spread, and her hand was shaking.

Brand was out within seconds, saw what had happened, asked: 'Have you spilt it on yourself?'

She shook her head. 'No, just the top. My hand slipped.'

'Better let me make it. Go and sit down.'

'No, I'll do it. I'll be more careful. It was a stupid accident.'

'Go and sit down, for God's sake!'

'I'm all right!' she flared, forgetting all the good intentions, the truce—everything.

'Then why the hell did you drop the kettle?' he demanded.

'I don't *know*! Don't you ever do anything wrong?'

'Not if I can help it.' Before she could move he had used the remaining water in the kettle to fill the beakers, added milk, put them to one side, found a cloth, and mopped the puddles up from the top. Maria, feeling vaguely like an unwanted spare part, stalked off into the living room, seething.

'Here,' Brand followed her in, handing her her coffee. 'Try not to spill that too.'

'You're so bloody clever, aren't you?' she blazed.

'Yes, I am,' he agreed in a manner so calm that it infuriated her more. 'And what happened to the pleasant truce we were enjoying?'

'Damn the truce,' she muttered, and he laughed.

'It didn't last long, did it?'

Icy-faced, she glared at him, hating him with every ounce of her. 'My God, but you've got a temper on you,' he drawled. 'You really have.'

'Coming from *you*, that's rich,' she retorted.

'Then it makes two of us. No wonder we strike sparks off each other.'

'Don't worry,' she breathed. 'In a couple of days we'll be away from here, and I won't have to see you again.'

'I wouldn't be too sure about that,' he answered calmly.

Maria caught her breath. 'What do you mean?'

'I said last night that I had something that we'd need to talk about today. Now is as good a time as any. Before I begin, are you going to listen, or do you want to hurl a few more insults at me first? If you do, go ahead.'

She was silent. There was something serious about his face that dissolved her remaining temper. 'Go on,' she said more quietly.

'There's the question of this house. It belonged jointly to my mother and your father. Did you know that?' She shook her head. 'No, I thought not. I only discovered it when I was reading the papers I found here before you came. I put them to one side. The question is, what happens next? Legally I suppose it would go half to me and half to your mother. Which leads to two questions. Did your father leave a will, and does your mother know about his relationship with my mother?'

'Oh God!' Maria groaned. 'Yes, he did leave a will, but this house wasn't mentioned. I suppose he thought if anything happened to him it would be your mother's. I just haven't thought about it. And to your second question—no, my mother didn't know, at least I'm sure not. But if she had, it—it wouldn't have mattered. She—leads her own life. I rarely see her.'

'I see. Well, I don't want it. I suggest we check up with some solicitors when we return to London. If he did leave it to my mother, I'll sign it over to you.' Brand's face was hard.

'No, I can't let you do that,' she protested.

'Why not?'

She shook her head. 'I can't, that's all.'

'You realise what you're saying?'

'That I don't want you to give it to me?'

'That I don't consider it mine in any way. You can keep the keys. You may want to visit it again.'

'No,' she said, 'I won't.'

'Why not? Because of the memories? If their love was so wonderful, shouldn't you want to come here——'

'*No!*' She put her hands to her face. 'Please stop. I don't know what to think—please, I don't want to talk about it.'

'I do. Then it will just be left to rot away. Is that what you'd like?' His voice was hard, relentless.

'No!' She jumped to her feet. 'Leave me alone— leave me——'

He stood up and grabbed hold of her hand. 'Stop living in a dream world, Maria. Grow up!'

She tried to pull her hand free, but without success. 'Let me go!' she gasped.

'No, I won't. Not until you calm down.'

She took a deep breath. 'I'm calm now.' But her face belied her words. She looked at him, and felt only contempt for the hard, heartless man that he was. She wished she were stronger, physically, she wished—she wasn't sure what she wished, she was only sure that she had never met a man she detested so strongly.

'You're not. You're practically hysterical.'

She made a supreme effort and wrenched herself free of him, and stood facing him defiantly. 'Don't use force on me,' she said, 'ever again.'

'You're childish and immature,' he said harshly. 'I'm talking about an important issue regarding the sharing of property and all you can do is fling yourself about and say you don't want to talk about it. What the hell am I supposed to do to make you listen?'

She had no answer to give him. She shook her head wordlessly. He had called her childish and immature, and perhaps he was right. Perhaps that was how she was behaving. But didn't he realise how he hurt her, stripping memories raw? Had he no feeling for the woman who had been his mother? She still missed her father dreadfully—yet would Brand ever understand that? She could only try.

'I'm sorry,' she said. 'I still feel very upset about—what happened. I felt dreadful at having to come here——' He stood there, no response, no understanding on his face, just listening to her words. 'Oh,' she went on, 'can't I make you see how awful it is for me to have to think about things like—what you're talking about?' She held up her hands in an unconscious gesture of appeal. 'Please believe me—please!'

There was a fractional softening of his hard features, no more than that. He's like a man of stone, she thought wretchedly. He denies love, he has no emotions at all. 'Then we'll leave it for the present,' he said. 'Drink your coffee before it gets cold. I'm going to go out for a walk. I need to get away for a while.'

Maria nodded. 'I can understand that.' She felt as if she wanted to get away too, right away from there. Brand glanced at the fire, growing low.

'I'll stoke up the fire before I go. I'll be about an hour.'

She lifted her head proudly. 'I can do that, don't worry. I know you think I'm clumsy, spilling the water, but it was an accident. I can get coal in. Is it in the shed at the back?'

'Yes, but I'll do it. You can't go lifting things in your condition.'

She managed a smile. 'I'm much better, and I'm not an invalid—only a little bruised. You're no lightweight, you know.' She put up her hand quickly. 'I wasn't saying it to remind you—I didn't mean *that*, believe me. I've not forgotten your remark about apologising every hour on the hour—I just meant it as a comment.'

Was it the faintest trace of a smile she could see on his face? A miracle if so. 'I know. The truce is on again, is it?'

'I think it had better be.' She looked directly into his eyes. 'But I must ask you this. *Have* you ever played rugby?'

'Only at college, and that must be fifteen years ago.'

'But it's like riding a bike, I suppose. You never forget.'

'Something like that.'

'I'm glad I wasn't a burglar.' Her words came from the heart.

'If I'd stopped to think about it. I'd have realised that no one in their right mind is going to travel by boat just to break into a remote cottage. They tend to go for easier pickings, and there's not another living soul on this island. But at four o'clock in the morning I suppose the mind isn't too clear about these finer points.'

'Probably not. If I'd eaten more during the day I wouldn't have been creeping round in the dark anyway.' Maria sighed. 'Still, what's done is done. Go for your walk, I'll wash up and get the coal.'

'Are you sure?'

'Quite sure.'

'I'll be no more than an hour,' he told her.

'You mean if you're not back in two I'm to send out search parties?'

'If you can find enough to make one up. Don't worry, I'll be back.'

He went to the door for his jacket and put it on. He looked at her as he opened the door. Cold air rolled in. '*Au revoir,*' he said.

'*Au revoir.*' The door closed softly and she was alone. It was a pleasant feeling to have. Or almost. She could relax at last, and sit by a good fire and adjust the lamp so as to be able to read by it, and when Brand came back it would be near enough time to go to bed.

She decided that after stoking up the fire she would have a good wash and change into the long kaftan she had brought. It was a fine wool garment, in deep blue, that packed like a dream, rolled into the corner of a suitcase, and never creased. She could relax by the fire, perhaps have another cup of coffee, put her feet up, and read.

Kneeling by the fire which now roared satisfyingly up the chimney, Maria turned the liniment bottle on its side to warm properly. She had decided to put another, more thorough application on while she could do so in privacy and, more important, in a warm room. The bedroom had been cold before. It was a mere fifteen minutes since Brand had gone. She had—safely— at least another quarter of an hour, and almost certainly three quarters, before he returned. It was dark outside now, but she had seen him take a torch with him. To ensure privacy, she had drawn the bright orange curtains and bolted the front door, and that would give her a few moments' grace if he did return unexpectedly.

She stripped to her pants and looked dispassionately at the bruises which were slowly but surely emerging. Her arms seemed to be the worst affected, and her shoulders, but there was a large darkening patch on one thigh. She sighed. Any self-respecting house-breaker would probably have sworn off burglary for ever after an experience with Brand Cordell. Brand— the name, as she looked at herself, seemed remarkably appropriate. She was undoubtedly branded. It was almost funny, and if she hadn't disliked him so much it would have been pleasant to share the joke with him. There was unfortunately no one else she could tell.

She opened the bottle and began smoothing the warm brown liquid on to her shoulders. The sharp pungent odour tickled her nostrils, and she sneezed. 'Ouch,' she muttered, finding another hitherto undiscovered tender patch on her upper arm. She smoothed over it gently. It prickled a bit at first, but then soothed. She turned her back to the fire and tried to reach her shoulder blades. 'Aah—ooch!' she winced with the effort of reaching her arm up. Both were still stiff and sore, but the exercise was good for her she knew. She just wished it didn't hurt so much.

'What's——'

She jerked in alarm, nearly sending the bottle flying, as Brand's voice came—from the doorway to the *kitchen*. She had forgotten the back door!

She tried to scramble to her feet, to reach her kaftan—but he was in the room and looking across at her. She froze in panic, and he stood there very still, and she saw that he held a radio in his hand.

'I came back to give you this from my Land Rover——' he began, never taking his eyes away from her, she said, quickly:

'Please turn away!'

He closed his eyes instead. 'Look, I didn't know——'

'Well, now you do,' she said fiercely. 'I didn't think you'd be *back*——'

'That's obvious,' he said in dry tones. He bent to put the radio on the floor, eyes still shut tightly, and Maria stood up and reached across for her dress and held it in front of her.

'You can open your eyes,' she told him, and he did so. 'I was putting on the liniment in a warm room because it's much easier.' Her face felt tight, and very warm.

Brand held up his hands. 'Why didn't you lock the door?'

'I did. I mean, I locked the front one—I forgot about the back.'

'Look, do you want me to put it on your back for you?'

'Not like this you can't.' She held the dress more securely in front of her.

'No, but if you wrap this round you instead,' he picked up the folded blanket from the settee and shook it out, 'like a sarong—then it can be done.'

She was tempted, very tempted. But could she trust him? It was one thing for him to reassure her when she was fully clothed, but he had just seen her practically naked. Maria wasn't a prude, but she was sensible.

'I won't touch you anywhere, or try to make a pass at you,' he said. 'Except to rub the liniment on your *back*. That is all.'

She swallowed. 'All right. Thank you.'

Brand handed her the blanket and turned away very deliberately. She wrapped it round her, tucked it firmly in place at the front and coughed.

'You can turn round now,' she said primly.

'So can you,' he said dryly, and bent to pick up the bottle. 'Now, where exactly? All over your back?'

'Yes. Er—just a moment.' She loosened the sarong-blanket slightly so that it dropped at the back to her waist. She kept her hands clasped firmly over her bosom. 'All right.'

His hands went across her shoulder blades in a smooth movement, then down slightly. He coughed. 'Wow, what a perfume!'

'Yes, it's terrible.' Her heart was thudding. She

hoped he couldn't hear it. His hand was very gentle, and he was massaging her shoulder blades, then he moved it to the nape of her neck, and the sensation—if she had allowed herself to relax—would have been wonderful. But she stood as if a statue, taut and tense, and he said:

'Look, you'll have to loosen your muscles a bit if you want me to do any good. I can massage your back properly—if you'll let me—but I can't when you stand like a board.'

'It's not easy for me, you know,' she said, in a rather strained voice. She cleared her throat. 'I mean——'

'I know what you mean,' he answered in extremely dry tones. 'I've just promised not to try anything.'

She tried, she really tried to relax, but it was difficult. 'Look,' he said, 'lie down on the floor, face down, in front of the fire. Let your whole body just go limp. I'll massage your back and your arms with both my hands—and if you want me to stop, just say so and I will.' His voice was completely impersonal. He didn't even like her, he had said so after all. Maria nodded.

'All right.' She took a deep breath. I'm quite mad, she thought, and another, inner voice murmured: 'But how wonderful it will be.' She silenced that very firmly and instantly.

Lying on the duvet a few moments later, respectably covered from waist to knees by the blanket, and with it covering her adequately underneath, she made a great effort to loosen her muscles. She felt Brand kneeling down. He had taken his jacket off while she lay down. Now, beside her, he asked: 'Are you ready?'

'Yes.' Her voice was muffled, her head turned away from him towards the fire.

'Okay. Stop me as soon as you've had enough.'

'Yes. I will.'

He began at the nape of her neck, both hands now,

one either side of her head, and it was immediately
apparent that he knew exactly what he was doing.
Maria found herself relaxing almost against her will as
the skilful strong fingers did their work. Down slightly
to her shoulders and upper arms, and what he was
doing, and what she had been doing, were worlds
apart. Her head swam with tiredness, so utterly
relaxed and soothed was she—but more—and she was
scarcely aware of it at the beginning in the first few
minutes, but then she was, very well aware. The touch
of his hands was sensual, there was no other way to
describe it. Utterly and completely sensual—yet when
he spoke, his voice was cool, very impersonal.

'Still okay? I'm not hurting you, am I?'

'No.' She could not trust herself to say more than
that. She dared not. Brand was having an odd effect
on her. She was filled with terrible sensations that
frightened and dismayed her and her heart pounded
and her head swam, not with tiredness now, but with
something else. She wanted him to stop. He must
stop—but she didn't want him to. She dug her nails
into the duvet to stop herself from screaming, the next
moment he tapped her hand lightly.

'Relax,' he said. Did he know? Could he know?
Surely not. She kept her hands flat. He had reached
her ribs now, and his hands were along her spine, then
across, each side, and she thought she would die. She
bit her lip hard; he couldn't see that.

'Nearly finished now,' he said, and she was sensitive
to any nuances there might be in his voice, and there
were absolutely none. His tone was totally impersonal,
almost flat.

Then, horror of horrors, she felt his hands on the
calf of her leg, froze, and heard him say: 'You've got a
beauty coming up there.'

She heard the clunk of the bottle as he picked it up.

She tried to speak but couldn't. To protest, to tell him to stop—but he took her silence for assent and moved slightly, and the next moment was massaging the backs of her legs.

'I never realised exactly what I'd done,' he said. 'My God, no wonder you were dropping things all over the place!' She heard his indrawn breath. 'You're a mass of bruises.'

'I know.' She was past caring about what was happening. The effect on her was too devastating for words—but equally obviously there was none on him. As why should there be? No reason at all. Maria was trembling; she hoped he wouldn't notice, because there was absolutely nothing she could do about it.

'Turn over,' he said briskly. 'I'll do the front of your legs, and your feet.'

'No,' she couldn't, she wouldn't. He would see her face . . .

'No? Okay. Lift your leg, so.' He lifted one slightly. 'I'll do it like this, then, one at a time.'

That was better. Easier. Legs were impersonal really—— 'If I sit up would you just do the back of my neck again?' she asked. Sitting up would be all right, safe. And facing away from him. Give her time to recover—and her neck was stiff, and he had done a lot of good. It might just sort it out properly.

'Yes, if you wish.' Gravely formal, absolutely cool. He was *cool*.

Maria kept her back towards him and eased herself up and sat crosslegged, facing the fire, and pointed her hand.

'Just—*there*.'

'Got it. Sit still.'

She intended to. Very still, very cool—like him. He knelt behind her, and he was, of course, higher up, so that his voice came from above. He laid his hands on her shoulders and began to work his way inwards, slightly upwards, warm, deep, moving slowly, beautifully to the nape of her neck. Her hair was swept round to her front, her long smooth dark hair, then his fingers were higher, where the hair started to grow, and stroking her scalp till it tingled. She tingled. She tingled all over and she couldn't breathe.

'That's——' she croaked. She tried to say 'that's enough,' but she couldn't quite manage it.

She felt his head near to hers, his voice almost a whisper in her ear, his breath on her cheek. 'That's what?' he said. 'I'm sorry, I didn't hear what you said.'

She couldn't move, she couldn't speak. Brand stilled his hand, the one in her hair, and then, gently, turned it so that she was nearly facing him. She looked up at him, and he saw what was in her eyes before she could close them and whispered: 'Dear God!' then he kissed her.

Maria was unaware that she was moving, lifting her arms to put at his neck, or that the blanket slipped down as she did so. She only knew that she had been waiting for him to do this since the first moment she had met him. She knew nothing else, only that what was happening was as inevitable as a heartbeat. It was an infinitely sweet and beautiful kiss that had no time to it. It was as though it never began and never ended. It just was. Brand's mouth was soft and sensual, as gentle as his hands had been, and still were, moving softly across her shoulders, to her neck, to cup her face as they tasted the sweetness of each other's lips. Nectar and honey and sweet breath mingling, and heartbeats touching.

She lay in his arms on the floor, and he kissed her again, and this too was timeless and formless, a blurring of the senses, with soft movements that had no beginning or end or reason, but were.

She was not aware of anything save Brand. She saw his face above hers in the blurred moments between each kiss, and his eyes were soft and very dark, and his mouth said silent words she couldn't hear, and his skin was smooth and dark because the light was far away, only flickering to throw shadows. Two bodies blended, four arms enfolded.

But then, at a certain point, when it was almost too late, he rolled to one side and put his hand over his face, and Maria sat up, shaken, trembling.

He too sat up. Her body gleamed in the soft glow of the fire, and she pulled up the blanket. For several moments neither could speak, then Brand did.

'My God, Maria,' he muttered, and his voice shook, and he was husky. 'That wasn't what I intended, I swear it.'

She closed her eyes. Her head throbbed painfully. 'I know,' she whispered.

He stood up and helped her to her feet. His hands had a fine tremor to match her own. He was visibly struggling for control, his breathing harsh and uneven, his eyes dark, face pale. His forehead was beaded with sweat.

'I need a drink,' he said, and sat down on the settee.

Maria went behind it and slipped her dress over her head, fastening the tie-on belt. Then she went into the kitchen and fetched in the bottle of whisky and the two glasses.

Brand drank his in one swallow and sat looking at the empty glass like a man only semi-conscious. Maria couldn't sit down. She sipped hers standing up and looked anywhere but at him.

'Look at me,' he said. 'Please.'

She looked then. 'I've never lost control like that before,' he said. 'I apologise. I despise myself for what just happened. It was entirely my fault.' His face was still white, and it was clearly an effort for him to speak at all.

Maria shook her head. 'I was as—foolish as you. Don't blame yourself.' She looked at the crumpled duvet on the carpet. 'Nothing happened.'

'It damn near did.' He put his glass in the hearth and his hands to his face.

She felt a welling surge of such anger that she couldn't contain it any longer. She stepped across to him and took hold of his hair and jerked his head back so that he was forced to look up at her. 'Yes, it did,' she said, her voice shaking with sobs, tears coming down her cheeks. 'I hate you! Do you hear me—I *hate* you!' She let go of his hair and swung away from him. 'Don't ever touch me again.'

As he got to his feet she turned to face him. Her mouth opened, she tried to speak, but couldn't, and her body shook as the tears came. Brand came towards her, and she, blinded by scalding tears, lashed out and hit him, then again, pummelling his chest with her fists. 'I hate you!' she sobbed.

He didn't move, or try to defend himself, and she stopped, put her hand to her mouth, and ran blindly out of the room and up the stairs.

# CHAPTER FOUR

MARIA lay in bed, still dressed in the kaftan, and gradually, as the minutes passed, she grew slightly more calm. Although her thoughts were chaotic, her emotions raw, she began to regain control of herself.

She was deeply ashamed of all that had happened— but in her innermost heart she knew that Brand Cordell had been no more to blame than herself. Yet she had lashed out at him in a terrible, uncontrollable anger, had wanted to hurt him. The memory of his face was etched on her brain as he stood there, not defending himself against her, just standing there, like a man tortured beyond endurance. She took a deep, shuddering breath and held tightly to the pillow that she clutched to her, her nails digging into it in her pain.

She must not stay here any longer, that she now knew with absolute clarity. She must go, get away from the house as soon as possible while she was still able to do so. Wide-eyed, she stared at the window. It was misty outside, the faint outlines of the trees no longer clear. Low tide would be some time around five in the morning. It was only ten, or just past, now. Her work here was nearly done. There were a few more papers, but she knew where they were, could take them and go, and read them when she got home. Her father wouldn't wish her to stay, not now, not after what had so nearly happened.

She had to stay awake. If she fell asleep there was the danger that she wouldn't wake up in time. And if she stayed until tomorrow then that might turn out to be too late. She willed herself to feel calmer and more rational, and gradually succeeded. And she began to think, really think deeply about her life, and herself, for the first time since her father had died.

Some part of her had died that day, three months previously. Her mother, a Shakespearean actress, had been touring in Australia at the time, and hadn't even come home for the funeral. All arrangements had been left to Maria, who had behaved like an automaton, calm, organised, so that her friends had remarked on it—had wondered at how little she had been affected. How could they ever know? She had been so hurt that life hadn't really mattered any more. Tony, who said he loved her, had been warm and sympathetic, but even he hadn't guessed her true feelings. Gradually she had begun to pick up the pieces, knowing only that one day soon she would have to come here to the house to sort everything out.

They had come here three times a year, always travelling separately, as she and Brand had done the previous day. It was one reason why there had been no breath of scandal when the accident had happened. A multiple pile-up on a notorious stretch of road, two separate cars—no connection between the woman in one, the man in another. Maria sat up, fighting back the tears. Only she had known the secret, and kept it, until yesterday when she had met Isobel's son, and seen his anger and felt his intense contempt for her father. There was no way, after that, that she could ever have liked him. And yet—she held the pillow tightly—and yet even then, through the dislike, she had been more intensely aware of him as a man than she had ever been with any other, even Tony.

She had known Tony for a year. He worked in another advertising agency, and he was good company, tall, attractive, even sexy—she was fond of him, she enjoyed going out with him, kissing, and being kissed by him, but neither he nor any other man had ever roused deep feelings within her.

Restless, she got out of bed and crossed over to the window to look out over a mist-swathed island. She traced a pattern on the glass with her finger. She had known about her father and Isobel for some time, had known, been shocked at first, and then accepted. She had recognised with some deep feminine instinct that the love they had for each other was rare and special—and in a way this had affected her relationships with men that she met. Love like that *was* possible, it wasn't only something that happened in magazine stories. It was like a brightness in a dark world, touching and lighting everything near. She would know it when—if—it ever happened to her. But it never had. Tony was kind, warm and caring, and they respected each other. Maria knew that he loved her, but she could only feel for him a pleasant affection, no more.

It wasn't fair to him, letting him go on hoping. When she returned home she would tell him so, and they would part as, she hoped, friends. This she had decided only since the savagery of what had happened downstairs so recently. She had glimpsed in herself for the first time the capability of raw, intense passion. It had taught her something, but she wasn't sure what yet, except perhaps one thing—that if she stayed, she and Brand would make love. It was possible to dislike a man intensely and yet want him. As she admitted that terrible thought, she closed her eyes in despair, and stood still, cold and aching, by the window. At last she had spoken the inner truth, and it was painful. It was also the reason why she had to get away.

Then, and only then, did she move. She stripped, shivering, and dressed in her warm clothes, then found her case and packed it. She made the bed neatly, laid suitcase and handbag on top, and settled down until Brand was asleep downstairs. She could hear him moving about, and knew with absolute certainty that he would not come upstairs. There was no truce now, there was nothing between. There was such a world separating them as to be completely unbridgeable. Brand was more of a stranger now than he had been when she arrived.

She crept to the door and opened it very slowly so that it made no sound, then listened. She heard his footsteps, saw him pass the foot of the staircase and go into the kitchen and she froze, but he never looked up. Then she heard the back door open and his footsteps outside. Her coat was downstairs, on the hook by the door. She had to get that before she left. She needed it to put on while driving, and waiting to leave. Where was he? Did she have time? Quickly, quietly, she crept down the stairs. He wasn't in the kitchen, and the back door was open. Heart in mouth, she ran across the living room, snatched her coat off the hook and ran back and up the stairs. She made it just in time. As she reached her bedroom she heard the back door slam shut.

Breathlessly she waited, heard Brand's footsteps in the kitchen, the clatter of the kettle, a cupboard door being opened. She could breathe again. She put her coat on and went over to sit on the bed. The next few hours would be the longest of her life, sitting in the darkness just waiting until she was sure he was asleep. He hadn't bolted the back door—that was something. The bolt was a large one, and needed strength. It would be easier. Ears keenly attuned, she sat waiting, and waiting . . .

She awoke from a doze and was horrified to think she had slept at all, sitting up against her bedhead as she had been, and she was stiff and cold. It was too dark to see anything, even her watch, but she had matches in her bag. Lighting one, she saw that it was nearly three. Time to go. The house was in darkness, and all was silent. She would drive down to the shore and wait there for the right moment to cross the causeway.

She picked up her case and bag, crept to the head of the stairs and waited. Silence. Darkness. One step at a time and pause, each step accomplished with great care, she descended. She could hear Brand's deep breathing from the living room, the breathing of someone fast asleep. There was a brief moment as she remembered . . . then she shivered, put it out of her mind, and crossed the kitchen. She had to put her case and bag down so as to open the door in silence. When it was open she put her things outside, stepped out, and closed the door, again with infinite care.

She took a deep breath of relief as that was accomplished. The worst was over. Damp misty air touched her face. It was cold and the paved yard was slightly slippery and the earth, when she reached the car, was hard and crunchy with frost. She wiped the outside of her windscreen with her hand, opened the door and got in, putting case and bag beside her. Praying that the car would start first time, she put the key in the ignition and turned it. Her trusty Mini had never let her down. Please don't let this be the first time it does, she said, heart in mouth. The engine throbbed into life. Maria grinned in relief, and, putting the engine into first gear, bumped slowly away down the track. Brand had backed her car into the parking space. For that she felt absurdly grateful to him. If she had had to back out it would have been twice the problem. As it was she drove slowly, carefully away from Rhu-na-Bidh and each moment that passed was one more to escape.

There would be a wait on the beach, she knew. The mist was growing thicker all the time, which was a worry, but if it were as bad, or worse, on the mainland, she could park somewhere until morning came when it would be bound to lift. The main thing was to get away from the island. Even if Brand discovered her gone, as he would when he woke up, there would be absolutely nothing he could do about it until mid-afternoon. Not that he would want to do anything about her departure. Why should he? His only feeling would be one of relief. She realised that she had been thinking about him as a captor, which was absurd. She was getting away for her own peace of mind, that was all. She shook her head; I'm mad, she thought. I should have just walked out, told him I was leaving. She was nearly at the beach now. The sea was calm, and she could only see a few yards ahead before mist obscured everything. But it was enough for her to know when the tide was right. It would be another hour at least. She switched off the engine and prepared to wait.

It would have been better if she had left him a note, if only to say she had gone, but it was too late now—or was it? She could write one, leave it somewhere on the shore—no, that was absurd. It would rain, or it would be blown away before morning. Maria gripped the steering wheel tightly. She had been stupid, running away like this, in the middle of the night when all she had to do was walk out in the middle of the afternoon. Brand couldn't stop her. He had expressed concern because of his attack on her, but she was much better and able to move, after his massage——She checked her thoughts. *That* was, after all, why she had left now. In panic after what had happened, nothing else. And because she no longer trusted herself.

It was uncomfortable and cold sitting in the car, but

it ensured that she remained wide awake. Her breath misted the windscreen; patterns formed, patchy and vague. She saw little save a grey blur outside, but she was patient, she could wait, and when she had reached the mainland she would be free of him for ever. He wanted her to have the house. It didn't matter, because she would never come here again. The house would remain, and each year that passed it would die a little more, and one day there would only remain a shell of stone.

She would go back to her job, and live her life, start anew, perhaps move house, travel more, see the world. She had never wanted to before, but perhaps now was the right time for change. She sighed. If she had come a few days earlier, or a few days later, it would have been sad, but she would still have been the same inside. Now, something was different. She wasn't the same person any more. She felt raw, aching, but intensely aware, as if she had woken up after a long sleep and was looking at the world through new eyes.

She switched on her headlights and they beamed a path over the water, so far, no farther, but enough to see that the level was lower, the tide receding.

Soon would be the right time. Very soon. Maria rubbed her hands together to restore the circulation and heard a man's voice call her name.

Instantly, panicking, she switched on the engine ready for flight. She looked round as the engine throbbed into life, and saw the large shadowy figure emerging out of the gloom behind her. Without thinking she changed gear to first, and the car rolled forward. She felt the bang on the back of the car as he tried to hold it and filled with unreasoning terror, shot forward as she accelerated.

The next moments were confused. If she had been thinking logically it would have been all right. The water was a mere few inches over the precious path, but her numbed hands slipped from the wheel, the car tilted, paused, then there was a grinding wrenching noise, she was flung sideways against the door and as she saw stars, heard the ominous lapping of water. Her last conscious thought was that she was going to drown—then she knew no more.

She drifted up through the layers of unconsciousness to a vague awareness of warmth and light. That was all, at first. Then other things swam into focus—the hard settee beneath her back, soft warmth above her, damp hair about her face. She lifted her arm to feel the duvet covering her, then pushed her hair away from her eyes. She was in the living room, lying on the settee covered in blankets and duvet—and she was naked.

She managed to sit up, and saw her clothes draped over the rocking chair by a roaring fire. Of Brand there was no sign. She pulled the underneath blanket more closely around her and swung her feet to the floor. They too were bare. Her throat ached, her body ached, she felt wretched—and sick.

Then his voice came, and she had to look round to see him standing at the kitchen doorway. It was obvious even from the beginning that he was angry, but how deeply and intensely was only revealed by his words.

'I should have left you to drown!' His voice was shaking. 'I can't even trust myself to be in the same room as you any more. I'd like to shake you senseless.'

He moved to stand in front of her. White-faced, he stared down at her and she pulled up the blanket in an instinctive gesture of self-defence. Brand reached out, brought her to her feet, and shook her hard. Then he flung her back and she, frozen with absolute terror, grabbed at covering and put the blanket over her. His violence shocked more than hurt her.

'I was leaving,' she gasped, almost too frightened to speak.

'Well, you're not bloody well leaving now, even if I have to tie you up—and I will, don't think I won't. You're absolutely crazy——' He stopped, and turned abruptly away to smash his fist on to the table, which rocked violently. He turned back to her. 'Did you *know* what you were doing? Hadn't you seen the weather?'

'If you hadn't come after me like that——' Maria began.

'Shut up!' he thundered. 'Or by God, I'll do it for you. Just don't speak, don't answer me back. Don't do *anything*. You're stupid beyond reason! You tried to drive away when you couldn't even see three feet in front of you——'

'I went because of *you*!' she cried, unable to keep silent. '*You*—don't you know why?' She was shaking uncontrollably now, but so frightened that in a way she was beyond normal fear. She began to weep, gasping, wrenching sobs that tore her apart. She hugged the duvet to her and rocked back and forth, and with the tears came a kind of release from the intolerable tension. She lay back exhausted after several minutes, to find herself alone.

She looked down at herself. Brand had stripped her while she had been unconscious. Fragments of memory began to return. The sensation of the car sliding sideways into the water, turning on its side—the sea rushing in with a scaring sound that had been terribly frightening—movement, hands that fought to release her from her seat belt, pushing, pulling—then the merciful blankness. And now this. Brand had saved her life. He had the right to be angry.

'Put these on.' Something was flung at her. 'I'm going back to see if I can get your case out. Stay there.' She watched him go out of the front door and held up the sweater and jeans he had thrown at her. Her pants were nearly dry. She put those on, then the sweater, finally the jeans. Both were miles too big. She rolled up the sweater sleeves, and the legs of the jeans, then sat down again.

Her hair was still soaking and she knelt carefully by the fire to dry it, gradually growing warmer as each moment passed. Outside it grew faintly lighter, still with mist, but it was nearly morning now, and she was trapped with Brand. There was no escape any more. She wondered how long she had been unconscious. Minutes? Hours? No way of telling. She folded the bedding and crept out to the kitchen, ready to flee back if she heard him returning. She was feeling stronger every minute, amazingly enough.

She filled the kettle and lit the gas. What was Brand doing? Would *he* be all right? She should have stopped him going back. The tide could be coming in again— he could be trapped—it was only clear for an hour, no more. Visions of him struggling in the water came to her, and fear, of a different kind, filled her and she went dizzy with it. Nothing must happen to him. She couldn't wait here not knowing. He had told her to, and was angry enough to strike her if she disobeyed, but what if he didn't come back? What if he was in trouble, and all because of *her*?

Maria switched off the gas and walked into the living room, consumed with fear and worry now. She found her sodden shoes and put them on, hitched the belt of the jeans tighter, and went out of the front door into the thick damp misty morning.

Blinded by tears, she ran full tilt into him. The collision jarred her so much that she couldn't speak for a moment. He had dropped her case and bag on impact and he grabbed her arm. 'I told you to stay put,' he grated. 'You stupid bitch!'

'I thought you were in danger—I was frightened—I had to come, I *had* to——' she gasped, then, without being aware of what she was doing, scarcely conscious of it, she flung her arms round him. 'Brand, I was so frightened for you.' She shivered uncontrollably. He was soaking wet. He made no move to push her away, he stood perfectly still, like a man in a state of shock, one who has lost the power to move. Slowly, tremulously, Maria lifted her head away from his chest.

'You're drenched,' she said, voice trembling. 'Oh, Brand, please don't be angry. I was frightened, so frightened for you——' She stopped, was aware that she had given herself away. Brand looked down at her then. He looked as though he was about to collapse. His face was almost grey. 'Come back,' she said, and took hold of his arm. 'Please. I'll collect the case later.'

He began to walk towards the house and Maria held his arm. It was as though he wasn't even aware of it. He looked dazed. They went into the house and she said: 'You'd better get your clothes off. The kettle's been on, I'll make you a hot drink.'

The anger had certainly gone, and in its place was something infinitely more disturbing. She would have preferred the anger. Brand looked ill.

He sat down on the settee and she moved the blankets to one side so that they wouldn't get damp. It was as though he hadn't seen her. Maria went to make tea, and when she returned he was still sitting where he had been. It was then that she saw the gash on his forehead. The blood had nearly dried, and the wound was just beneath his hairline by his temple, about three inches long. She looked at it for a moment before speaking.

'How did you cut yourself?' she asked.

He looked up and took the beaker from her. 'What?' he asked.

She touched his forehead gently. 'There—the cut. You hurt yourself.'

'Did I?' He put his fingers up, then winced. 'The car—I must have banged my head getting the case out. I seem to remember——' he drank some tea. 'That's better. No wonder my head aches!'

'I'll clean it for you. Have you a first aid box in your Land Rover?'

'Yes, in the glove compartment. It's nothing——'

'Never mind. It should be cleaned. Drink that, I'll not be a minute.'

Maria went out. He might have concussion; it would explain his apparent docility after his monumental anger. If that were the case she would have to take care of him. She wished, wretchedly, that she had never tried to leave.

She put the kettle on again when she returned, and spent several minutes cleaning what turned out to be a shallow long cut with a bruise forming near it. She filled a hot water bottle and took it to her bedroom, put it in the bed and removed the pillow. Then she went down to him, took the empty beaker from him and said gently: 'Brand, you'll have to get your wet clothes off now.' She helped him to his feet. He was complaisant as a tired child. It was not going to be easy, she knew that, but it had to be done. She stripped off his soaking wet pullover and shoes, told him briskly and firmly to take off his trousers, and turned her back.

'Have you done?' she asked.

'Yes.'

'Then put a blanket round you,' she ordered. When she ventured to turn he was standing, blanket-wrapped. He put his hand to his head.

'My head——' he began.

'I know. Come up to my bed and rest for a while until your headache goes. I've put a hot water bottle in, you'll be warm.' She grabbed the duvet as she guided him out and up the stairs. She opened the covers, moved the bottle aside, and helped him in, tucking him in firmly. 'Better?' she asked.

'Yes.' He smiled faintly. 'Don't go.'

'I won't.' In fact, she intended to stay to keep him awake until she could be sure his injury was not dangerous.

'I'm cold,' he said after a while. He shivered. But he was alert now, no longer dazed. 'Cold,' he repeated. 'So cold.'

'Wait,' Maria said softly. Pulling the covers away, she slid into bed beside him and lay down, putting her arm round him. He lay on his side facing her, and gave a deep sigh.

'That's better,' he said. 'Much better.'

'Then sleep,' she whispered. She intended to wait until he did. She hadn't intended to fall asleep herself. But that was what happened.

She awoke wondering for the moment where she was. Then she looked at the man beside her, and remembered. She eased herself cautiously up on her elbow and looked at Brand's sleeping face. He looked better, no longer grey, but only slightly pale. His breathing was normal, and he was warm.

Maria let out her breath in a silent sigh of relief. She had been terribly worried about the abrupt change in his behaviour before, even more concerned when she had discovered the reason, and now, at last, she felt the warm surge of relief that filled her. She looked at him, taking everything in, the smooth tanned skin, the darkening shadow round jaw and mouth, the closed eyes with the thick dark lashes, broad mouth and nose, strong face. A man quick to anger, potentially violent—and the man who had saved her life. The man that she loved. The man she now knew she loved in a way she had never imagined possible. If anything had happened to him that morning she would have wanted to die herself.

'Oh, my dear,' she whispered silently so that not even he would hear. It was time for her to go. Easing herself out of bed, she was about to move away when he woke up.

'You're all right,' she said softly. 'Just stay there, I'll get you a drink.'

Brand frowned, then winced. 'What happened?'

She sat on the bed. 'You got a nasty knock when you were trying to save my luggage. I put you in my bed. Don't try and talk too much. Are you hungry?'

'Starving!'

'Then I'll get you something to eat as well.'

'I'm coming down,' he announced.

'No, not yet——'

'*Yes*. I don't have much choice.'

'Oh!' She went pink. 'Then take it slowly. Oh! You've—er—no clothes on. Wait there, I'll see if they're dry.'

'I've got pyjamas in my case. I rarely wear them, but I brought a pair.'

'I'll get them.' She fled. She knew where his suit-case was downstairs. She took it up and opened it for him. He took out severe blue pyjamas and an exotic jazzy dressing gown. 'Can you manage?' she asked.

'Yes. I'll be down in a few minutes.' She put the case by the window and left him alone.

Her own clothes were dry and she changed quickly into them, then went to prepare a meal for them both.

Brand seemed a little better after taking a bowl of beef broth down by the fire, which Maria had replenished with coal. The temperature outside the house was near freezing level, and the mist which had begun over-night now was a blanket that deadened all sound. They were truly isolated in that small house on the island. There was not the slightest possibility of get-ting away while the deadening mist stayed—Which was one reason why she was thankful Brand hadn't been more badly hurt. For there would have been no opportunity of getting help if he had needed it. For a few minutes that morning she had experienced a cold dread that he would need a doctor, that he was suffer-ing from severe concussion. The relief was great; she felt almost lightheaded with it. While still quiet and subdued, he had most of his colour back; it was enough for the moment. She knew the importance of rest for him, and warmth—and no stress.

Now, incredibly, she was the strong one. A great calm had come over her. After the shattering events of the early morning, she had thought a great deal about everything. She thought about the realisation of the love she felt for Brand, an alien feeling, that had, as it were, stolen up on her and caught her by surprise. It had never happened to her before, and she had not imagined that it would be like this. Startling, sudden—a look—and then the knowledge flooding her very being. She had no illusions about him. She knew that in two days, maybe less, maybe more, they would go their separate ways and never meet again. There was no possibility that Brand could share what she felt. For one reason that he scorned the very word—for another, more basic, because of the circumstances in which they had met. Maria accepted this with the calm part of her that even now was planning how best to care for him. She had no thoughts for herself, only for him.

She took the empty bowl from him and fetched in a basin filled with warm water, and his soap, washcloth and towel. 'I thought you might like to wash your face and hands,' she said. 'It'll make you feel fresher.'

He looked up at her. 'Thank you.'

Maria knelt in front of him and laid the towel over his knee, placed the bowl on the carpet and wrung the washcloth out in it. After rubbing soap on it she handed it to him. 'There, wipe your face first,' she said.

He did so; docilely, no fire or aggression now. 'I didn't shave today,' he said, rubbing his jaw.

'Never mind. Tomorrow will do.'

'You're not a nurse in your spare time, are you?'

She smiled. 'No. Do I seem like one?'

'Yes—efficient and bossy.'

'Thanks.' She bobbed a curtsey. 'You've been in the wars. The least I can do is look after you. You saved my life this morning.'

'Did I? It seems rather hazy.' He handed her the washcloth. 'That's fine. What next?'

'Bed.'

'It's only—— What time is it?'

'About six. My watch has stopped. You might have concussion, so it's best for you to rest. You'll be fine tomorrow.'

Brand looked at her and for a moment she caught a glimpse of the old hardness. 'You even sound like a nurse!'

'I know. Just pretend I am, it'll make it a lot easier.'

His mouth twitched. 'I don't have much choice, do I?'

'You're feeling better now, obviously. There's a faint touch of the aggression I was getting used to.' Her smile softened the words.

He touched the plaster that covered the wound on his forehead. 'This is bloody stupid, you know,' he said. 'I should have allowed for the angle the car was at, but I didn't. I remember it now——'

'Look, don't talk, don't even think about it, all right? You've had a nasty knock, but you're fit and healthy and you'll soon be better——'

'I'm not an invalid, and I don't need humouring,' he told her flatly.

'I didn't say you were.' She picked up the basin. 'I'll go and empty this.'

'I'm never ill. Never.' He stared at her as if challenging her to deny it. Maria sighed. The wash had been more effective than she could have imagined. He was getting back to normal with a vengeance.

'I'm sure you're not,' she answered with a touch of asperity. 'So why don't you go for a ride on the bike just to prove it?'

'There's no need to be sarcastic!'

She laughed and walked out. She loved him? She *was* mad. Brand followed her into the kitchen. 'I'm not going to bed now for you or anybody. Where am I sleeping, anyway?'

'Upstairs in my bed. It's more comfortable than the settee.'

'And you? Where will you sleep, then?'

'I can manage down here.'

'I see. I'll go to bed later. I'm going to read——'

'No, you're not.'

'Really? Who says?'

'I do. That's the most stupid thing you could do with concussion——'

'I've had a crack on the head, I'm not concussed.'

Maria took a deep breath. She must not argue; she must *not*. 'No, I'm sorry, I didn't mean that. But you have had a bump, you could get a bad headache if you read a book—I'll read to you if you want.'

'Will you? Where, down here?'

'Yes, by the fire. Whatever you want me to read.'

'Okay.' He walked away from her. She glared at his

back, then flung the washcloth in the sink. Something told her he was not going to be the ideal patient. Docile? Had she thought him *that?* She counted to twenty slowly, then went back to join him in the warm and comfortable room.

# CHAPTER FIVE

MARIA realised after an hour that Brand had fallen asleep. She put the book down quietly and stifled a yawn. Now at last she could have something to eat without worrying about him. She crept out to the kitchen and made herself a sandwich and heated the remains of the broth, then ate the meal out there. A blank greyness lay beyond the windows, and the kitchen was cold.

She filled the kettle and refilled Brand's hot water bottle, then went in to rouse him. She shook his arm gently. 'Brand, time for bed!'

He woke and looked indignantly at her. 'I thought you were reading to me. You said you would.'

'I was, but you fell asleep.'

'I didn't. I was listening.'

She was not going to argue with him. Not at all. Not ever again. 'Oh, I'm sorry. Look, if you go up to bed I'll come up and read there, then if you feel tired I'll stop. How's that?'

'I can't get to sleep until I've had a shave.' Maria stifled a sigh, resisting the temptation to roll her eyes heavenwards.

'I can't shave you.'

'It's a battery one,' he told her. '*I* can.'

'Oh, well, of course, that's all right. Let's go up and I'll fetch it. Where is it?'

'In the bathroom.'

She gave him a bright smile. 'Right. I'll give you a mirror as well.'

71

'You want me to go up now?'

'When you're ready.' She thought that loving him would have meant never feeling exasperated with him. It was not so. He was quite infuriating.

'Give me a few minutes,' he said. 'Can I have a cup of tea as well?'

'Of course. I'll make you one now.'

'And something else to eat. I'm still hungry.'

'What would you like?' she asked.

'Anything. A piece of toast—no, two, and—er—what is there?'

'Marmalade, potted beef, some cheese.'

'Potted beef and a piece of cheese.' She nodded, and gave him a bright smile. 'Right. Ready in five minutes. I'll do the toast on the fire.'

'Not too well done,' Brand said faintly. 'Nicely browned.'

'Nicely browned,' she repeated, teeth clenched to stop herself from screaming.

'Yes, please.' He walked slowly out towards the kitchen and paused on the way. 'I don't like Cheddar. It's not Cheddar, is it?'

'I don't bloo——' Maria stopped. 'I don't know. *You* bought it.'

'Oh. Did I? No, that's okay. It's Cheshire.' He went out and Maria banged her head with her fists and let out a heartfelt groan. Then she took a deep breath and went to find the bread and a fork.


'Right a bit—no, down, *down*! You've missed—see——' Brand pointed, lifting his chin up, and Maria gritted her teeth and bent over him and resisted the temptation to strangle him with her bare hands. He sat propped up in bed, mirror in hand, and allowed her to use his electric battery razor on him. She didn't see why he couldn't use it himself, but hers was not to question. She obeyed his every instruction and as she finished and he stroked his face she asked:

'Is that all right?'

'Yes, thanks. Now is the tea brewed?'

'Yes. I'll go and pour it out. Won't be a minute.'

Brand lay back as if being shaved had exhausted him. 'Take your time,' he said. 'There's no hurry.'

Maria could not believe that this was the same man who had greeted her with such hostility, who had, less than twenty-four hours later, nearly made love to her, and was now being the imperfect invalid. It was like meeting three different men. She felt totally confused. This one was undoubtedly the most maddening of all three. She poured out his cup of tea and a vague, half formed suspicion came into her mind. She dismissed it. No, of course not. It returned—not to be stifled so swiftly. Could Brand possibly be acting up? Could he possibly be secretly enjoying the situation of having an acquiescent woman attending to his every whim?

She walked quietly up the stairs and into the bedroom and looked at him. Brand lay with eyes shut. The gash was genuine enough. She had, after all, attended to it herself. He was pale, and he could hardly make himself so from choice. But was he really concussed, or just taking advantage of her natural guilt?

'There you are,' she said, and he opened his eyes and smiled faintly.

'Thanks.'

'It's my pleasure.' She sat on the bed. 'How do you feel now?'

He gave a wan smile. 'Fine.'

'You're very brave,' she said warmly.

'Am I?'

'Oh yes. A lot of people wouldn't be able to eat or drink in your condition. They'd be flat on their backs.'

Brand sighed, just a slight one. 'I'm not a lot of people.'

'How true.' She sighed too. 'You're a splendid actor for a start.'

'What?' He frowned.

Maria looked him straight in the eye. 'You're really enjoying yourself, aren't you?'

'I don't know what you mean.'

'Like hell you don't! You'd win an Oscar for the performance you've been putting——'

He groaned and clutched his head. 'I don't understand what you're saying——' he began.

'I think you do,' she retorted brightly.

'You're saying I made *this* up?' He indicated the plaster.

'No. But you're taking full advantage——'

'Of what? You?'

'I'm not grumbling, you understand,' she told him. 'I deserve it all. It was *my* fault you cracked your head, I'm well aware of that. I just wanted to let you know that I'm also aware that you're not as delicate as you'd like me to think.'

'In that case why did you sleep with me all afternoon? You did, didn't you?'

'Hold it,' she warned. 'Let's get it quite clear. When you say "slept" with you, you mean it in the literal sense of the word, I trust?'

'I can't remember anything happening, can you?'

She was beginning to wish she hadn't started this. 'No! I did it because you were cold, and feverish——'

'You just accused me of putting on an act,' he reminded her. 'Make up your mind.'

He looked at her. She looked at him. Their eyes clashed in the silent challenge, and his face was expressionless. Maria quashed a welling of anger. He was clever, she was reasonably sure he wasn't as ill as he pretended to be—and yet concussion was a delicate condition. She had not to anger him, however much she felt. She took a deep breath. 'I'm not going to argue with you——'

'That *would* make a pleasant change!'

She went on as though he hadn't spoken. 'Because you've had a knock on your head, I don't want to upset you, and I'll look after you until you're better because it's my fault. Just as long as I make myself clear, Brand, I don't mind.'

'You do, perfectly—and for the first time, Maria.' His face was hard. 'We seem to be stuck with each other, don't we?'

'For the moment, yes.'

'Just a couple of accident-prone lunatics. You nearly getting yourself drowned, me cracking my head. What next, I wonder?'

'You forgot the bit about you mistaking me for a burglar,' she put in dryly. 'And don't worry, I'll try to see there is no next time. I'm not going to make a dash for it again. When I go, it will be at the right time and in the right weather. I've checked the food situation and we have enough to last several more days with ease, and a week with care. There's a large tin of oatmeal downstairs. If we go on to porridge I dare say we'd survive a siege.'

'Can you make it?' he asked.

'I can do anything I want to,' she said, smiling prettily at him, wondering how she could have thought she'd manage to strangle him. He was built like a rugby player, thick strong neck. She wouldn't have even got her hands round it.

Brand sighed. 'I'm tired with all this talking. My head hurts. Can I have two aspirins?'

'I suppose so. I'll get them.' As she made to get up he caught her hand.

'Wait. Don't go yet.'

'I thought you wanted two aspirins——' She looked at the hand holding hers.

'I do. But how do *you* feel? I'm a selfish swine, letting you do all this when you're not so much better yourself after two nasty accidents in two days.'

'As a matter of fact I feel quite splendid,' she answered, with a fair amount of truth. The shock of seeing Brand ill, seeing the wound on his forehead, had jolted her completely out of any lingering traces of the after-effects of her near-drowning. She removed her hand from his. 'Can I go now?'

'No. I was wrong about you,' he added. 'You've got guts.'

'Thanks.' She stood up. 'Perhaps we've both been wrong about each other.' And so saying, she went out and left him to ponder that. Did he mean that he'd considered her a spineless, wishy-washy creature before? She had no intention of asking, of course, but she wondered about it. No, she thought, not that. He told me I made him angry. Spineless creatures don't make people angry, because they never argue. They're rarely noticed. She took a glass of water up with the aspirins and gave him two.

'As we're going to be stuck here,' he said, 'is there anyone who'll miss you—be worried, I mean?'

'Not for a couple of days. Why do you ask?'

'I wondered.'

'There's nothing we can do about it at present anyway, is there?' she pointed out.

'No. But would anyone come looking for you?'

'No one knows where I am.' She was puzzled about his line of questioning. What on earth was he getting at? 'Why? Will *you* be missed?'

'No. I often take off for days—weeks——' he shrugged.

'How nice,' she murmured. 'A gentleman of leisure.' She was wildly intrigued.

'Not exactly. Just—independent.'

'That's nice too. No nine-to-five office job?'

'No. And you?'

'Oh, I'm a working girl,' she told him.

'A nurse?'

'No.' She laughed. 'Hardly. I work in an advertising agency.'

'Really?' Brand looked surprised. 'Which one?'

'I don't think that's any of your business,' she responded levelly. 'Do you?'

'It might be. If it's Prothero and Michaels.'

She went cold, really cold for a moment. Brand saw by her expression that he had hit the nail on the head. 'So you do?' he said, and smiled faintly. 'How odd. Or perhaps not so odd after all.'

'Why did you ask? How did you know? You don't work there.'

'That's a matter of opinion isn't it? Whether I work, I mean——'

She still didn't know. All that she could think was that he must have worked there in the past—for she had been there two years since leaving college, and had never seen him. It was, admittedly, a large agency, with a branch in Manchester and one in Edinburgh, and many staff. But she knew everyone in her London branch, and Brand came from London.

'I've never seen you before, and I would have done.'

'I don't work *at* the office. I own the firm.' He said it so casually that it took a few seconds for the words to register—and then Maria didn't believe them. She stood up, feeling rather sorry for him for the first time, and, in a strange way, disappointed. Whatever else she had thought about him, it wasn't that he would be that rather pathetic kind of man, a braggart.

She nodded. 'Of course you do. Is there anything else you need? I have a few jobs to do downstairs.'

'You don't believe me, do you?'

'No. But I'm sure you enjoyed the little boast. I won't spoil it, I promise you. It'll be our little secret.' She put her finger to her mouth and made a shushing sound.

'My mother—Isobel's—maiden name was Prothero. The firm was founded in 1933 by her father, my maternal grandfather, with his cousin Ralph Michaels. He bought Michaels out shortly after, and when he died ten years ago, left the agency to my mother. I don't lie about my mother, Maria, I never have. She left the agency to me in her will.' He stared levelly at her. 'Well? Still sceptical?'

She shook her head, ashen-faced. 'I'm—sorry.' There was a chair in the room, and she went and sat on it, still digesting his startling information.

Brand pulled himself up in bed. 'So it won't matter if you don't go into work on Monday, will it? You'll be here, looking after your—employer.'

It seemed a deliberate hesitation on his part before saying the last word. Maria, sitting very still, knew now why she had found it so easy to get her present highly paid job there. It had been at her father's persuasion. Yet he hadn't said anything about Isobel owning the firm—for which she didn't blame him at all. She just wished she had known. She was happy there, had been for two years. She had surely never connected the mysterious—and never seen—'Miss Prothero' with her father's long-time love. A lot of women kept their maiden names for business purposes. She realised with a keen sense of loss that she could no longer remain there.

She nodded. 'So I will. And don't worry, when we do get back, I'll save you the trouble of sacking me. I'll hand in my notice.'

He lifted one eyebrow. 'Now why should you want to do that?'

'Don't play games, Brand. Or shall I call you "sir"? You're enjoying this, aren't you? I've no taste for working for you any more than you'll have for employing me. Or have you forgotten our reasons for being here?'

'I couldn't ever forget, could I? Nor what's happened since.' He gave a wry smile. 'But business is business. I assume you're competent, or you wouldn't have lasted five minutes. How long have you been there?'

'Two years.'

'A long time in advertising. You must be good.'

'What would you know about that? You've never even been in the office.'

'I own the firm because of my mother's death,' he reminded her. 'I've only owned it for a few months—I do have other interests. I didn't live off my mother, Maria. I have a career of my own.'

'I'm—sorry.' She felt wretched. 'But I'm still leaving.'

'As you wish. I can't stop you, of course.'

'That's true. Can I go now?'

'I can't keep you here either.' Brand turned his head away, as if in pain, and Maria stood up to leave the room. She went downstairs slowly, still shocked by what she had heard. She felt very sad. In the living room she tidied mechanically round, straightening cushions, poking the fire and adding more coal from the scuttle. Then she sat by the hearth and looked into the flames, allowing the memories to flood back. Memories of holidays with her father, walks in the country with him at weekends, their long talks about life, and the world. Their shared sense of humour, the fun he was to be with—— Tears filled her eyes. In the three months since he had died she had been living in an emotional vacuum. A light had gone from her life. And now, in the past few minutes, Brand Cordell had—almost certainly not deliberately—taken something else away from her. She looked up towards the mantelpiece, scarcely seeing anything. She had reached an impasse in her life. This, just now, although a cruel blow, was in a way a kind of watershed.

How she reacted now, what happened in the next few months, would probably set the pattern for her future life. She stood up and looked at herself in the mirror, and smoothed a speck from her forehead. She breathed deeply, steadily, and watched the reflection, the calm, serene face, looking slightly younger than her twenty-three years, that looked back at her. Since she had come here her life had been turned completely upside down. She had behaved in ways she was ashamed of, because of the man upstairs, she had been angered, she had been aroused in a way she could never have imagined, by him, and she had fought with him in an exhausting battle of personalities. Her friends—and she had many—would not have recognised her. 'Oh God,' she whispered, and put her face in her hands because she couldn't bear to look at herself any more.

There was no escape, not yet. She had tried it once, with many disastrous results, but she wasn't going to try again anyway. She would leave with dignity when the time came to go, and she wouldn't look back. In an odd way it was as if the house represented the past, and that was finished. The future was what mattered now; the present and the future. There would be another job. She would find one, perhaps after a brief holiday, and she would forget all about Brand Cordell. There was no other way to be.

She turned away from the mirror and went into the kitchen and found the bottle of whisky and a glass. She poured herself a small measure and raised the glass. 'To the new me,' she said, and smiled. Her father would have appreciated that. With his wonderfully outrageous sense of humour, he would have seen the funny side too, just as he did of most things. And so will I, Maria thought. Meeting him isn't the end of everything. Falling—unwillingly—in love isn't, either. So stop feeling sorry for yourself, you stupid idiot, and begin to live.

She sipped at the whisky and it went down warm and mellow; she coughed a little and exclaimed: 'Wow!'

Then she began to laugh. She laughed until the tears ran down her cheeks, then she saw Brand standing in the doorway and she laughed some more, and raised the glass. 'Cheers,' she said.

'Cheers,' he answered dryly. 'You seem to be enjoying a good joke. Er—have you drunk much?'

'Just this,' she answered. 'Just one. I'm not drunk, and I'm not mad, I'm laughing because I've seen the funny side of it at last.' She let out her breath in a deep sigh. 'Phew!' She smiled at him. 'And you helped.'

'Did I?' He walked over and poured himself a small tot into a clean beaker that was handy. 'I don't see how—but you obviously do. Would you like to tell me?'

'You wouldn't understand.'

'You can try me.'

'All right. When I knew who you were—my boss, I mean—and that I'd have to leave the job I loved, it was the last straw. Really the final blow—and I came down here and thought about it, and realised that in a way it was a good thing. I'd reached rock bottom after my father died, but at least I had my work, which I enjoyed—still do. Then you dropped the bombshell. I just decided, a few minutes ago, that I'm going to shake out of it, stop feeling sorry for myself, get back to living. So—thanks.' She finished the whisky in one neat swallow. 'See?'

'No, not exactly. You said one thing wrong—that you'd "have" to leave the job you loved. You said it upstairs too. There's no "have to" about it—just remember that. I wouldn't use my position as boss of the agency in any way like that.' Brand looked reflectively into the beaker. 'I may be many things, Maria, but I'm not that kind of swine.'

'I apologise. I really didn't mean that you would. I just can't stay, that's all. Let's put it that way. And as you said yourself, you can't stop me.'

'What do you intend to do?' he asked.

'Have a holiday, then find another job. And live.'

'Live? Haven't you been doing so until now?'

'Yes—but not in the way I'd wish. Anyway, you don't want to hear about me. Do you want anything?'

'I was going to make myself a coffee.'

'I'll do it,' said Maria. 'Go and sit down. I'll bring it in.'

'Thank you, I will.'

'How's the head?' she asked.

'Better, thanks.'

'That's good. I'm not sure if a doctor would allow you whisky, but I can't stop you.' She filled the kettle. 'I'm not your keeper.'

'You *are* my nurse.'

'No.' She shook her head. 'You don't need one. I'm not even sure you need looking after any more. You seem fine to me.' She looked at him and smiled gently. 'It's all right, though. I'll make your coffee and do what I can. I shan't shout at you or tell you off if you drink, or smoke or go for bike rides. You're as free as I am.'

'You *have* changed,' he commented wryly.

'Yes, I have. I've seen the funny side of everything at last. That's something I have my father to thank for. He made life seem richer, somehow, because of the way he looked at it.' She paused, and added: 'I don't think you would have hated him if you'd met him, Brand. He was a wonderful man and I'm proud to be his daughter.' She didn't know what made her add those words, but they were right, and they had been waiting to be said for too long.

He looked up very slowly from his beaker to meet her eyes. 'I'm sure he was. Perhaps I should have met him.'

'They—Isobel and he—they enriched each other's lives too. I know you don't accept that, and probably never will, because of the way you feel, but it's the simple truth. They were——' she hesitated, 'both better people for having known each other.'

She knew he didn't want her to have said it, but she had. She turned away from him and went to the cupboard for the beakers. She didn't want to see his face. It didn't really matter if it made him angry. She had said what she had to, and whether he accepted it or not didn't alter anything. She was pleasantly surprised at how calm she felt. It was as if all her previous anger and despair had drained away.

When she turned back from the cupboard Brand had gone. And when she carried the coffee in he was sitting by the fire, staring into the flames, and his face was drawn and pale.

'Brand?' She stood near him, ready to hand him the coffee. He looked up, and it was as if he had been a long way away.

'Yes? Oh, thanks.' He took the beaker from her. He looked as if something had hit him very hard. Maria sat in the rocking chair. Surely her words hadn't had this effect. He looked almost ill.

'Are you all right?' she asked.

He looked up from his contemplation of the fire. 'I'm—fine,' he said slowly.

'You're very pale.'

'I'm tired.' He touched the plaster. 'Perhaps I'm not as tough as I thought.'

'Perhaps it's hit you, as it were, belatedly. It happens. A good night's sleep will be the best thing.'

'It probably will. It's Sunday tomorrow, isn't it? I should think we could leave on Monday, don't you?'

'I hope so.' Maria suddenly remembered something. 'Good grief! My case—and my handbag. We left them.' She put down her beaker. 'Can I borrow your torch?' Then, very belatedly, she remembered something else. How could she have simply forgotten? 'And my car? Is it—is it in the water?'

'It was. You won't be able to drive it home, I'm afraid. It'll need a tow—which I can do tomorrow, I hope, to get it out—but I'm damned sure the engine will have had it.'

'Oh, my God! And I forgot, I completely forgot!'

'So did I. I'm sorry, but there it is.'

She stood up. 'My torch is on the dresser. Are you sure you'll be all right?'

'Yes, I will. I'll only be ten minutes.'

Maria put on her coat, took the torch, and opened the front door. A grey curtain of mist billowed in and she gasped, 'Oh, this is awful!'

Brand stood up, moving slowly like a man in pain. 'Wait! You can't go out in——'

'But my bag——' she protested.

'Is it as important as your life? No one's going to steal it.'

'No, I know, but——'

He closed the door firmly. 'You can't go out in this.'

'Are you forbidding me to go?'

'I can't do that, Maria. At the moment I don't feel strong enough. I'm just asking you to wait until the mist lifts a little.'

'But it's nearly ten now. It won't lift tonight. All my things are in my case——'

'Please,' he said. Just one word, but it held an agony in it, and she was stilled. She shrugged.

'All right, I'll leave it until tomorrow. Come and sit down again. I'll have my coffee with you and then I think I'll get ready for bed.'

Brand walked slowly over to the settee and sat down. Maria saw—and she was quite sure that he wasn't aware of it—the stiff way that he held his head, the tightening of a muscle in his jaw, as he sat down. She hadn't noticed it before, but it was as though his neck and shoulders ached.

She intended to watch and see if it was repeated, but not to mention it.

She picked up his beaker and handed it to him. 'Thanks,' he said. 'Now, you promise you won't do anything stupid after I've gone up to bed?'

'Such as what?'

'Such as going out quietly when I'm safely out of the way.'

Maria was silent. She was in fact more concerned in watching him and the way he moved than guilty at his question. Though she had planned to do just that.

He said more sharply: 'Is that what you plan?'

'Er——' she began, and stopped.

'Then I'll stay down here unless you give me your word.'

'You really mean it, don't you?' she said wryly.

'Yes, I do.'

She sighed. 'I promise. I won't leave this house for

any reason until morning.'

'And not even then if the mist is too heavy.'

'Yes, all right.' She sighed. 'Now, will you drink your coffee, please?'

'Yes.'

'You realise I'll have to sleep in these clothes?' she accused him.

'You'll be warmer.'

'I'm sure I will,' she said dryly.

'You can have a toothbrush,' he said. 'I always carry a spare—a new one, I mean.'

'That's a relief. You don't carry a spare pair of pyjamas as well, do you?'

'Sorry, no. You can borrow the top to these.' He grinned suddenly, and looked, for a moment, much better.

It was quite funny. 'No, thanks, but thank you for the offer.'

She stood up and went to take his now empty beaker. She knew, as he tried to look up, that her previous thoughts had been correct.

'Brand, does your neck hurt?' she asked.

'A little. It's nothing.'

She knelt down before him so that he wouldn't have to move his head.

'Let me rub it,' she said.

'No, it'll be all right. Thanks all the same.'

'Are you sure? You look as though you're in pain.'

'I'll live.'

'You're obstinate,' Maria sighed.

'I've been called that before.' Brand rubbed his neck and winced. 'Bloody hell!'

'And as stupid as you've accused me of being,' she snapped, exasperated with him. 'Can't stand the liniment, I suppose? Poor thing!'

He managed—with difficulty—to lift his head so

that he could glare at her. 'You're doing fine,' he grated. 'Getting your own back because I won't let you dash off out to get your case and break *your* neck?'

'I could hit you,' she murmured softly. 'I really could!'

'It wouldn't be the first time. Why don't you try it again? It might make my neck better. It'll certainly do a lot of good for my alleged concussion——'

'You are simply the most *maddening* creature!' she hissed, and slammed out of the room. You need more than a sense of humour to cope with men like him, she thought. You need the disposition of a saint. She shook her head and murmured: 'Give me strength!' silently and fervently to the kettle.

Then came a sound, as if of something being hurled against a wall, from the other room, followed by a muffled oath. Maria counted ten slowly and went in to see what he had done.

# CHAPTER SIX

MIDNIGHT at last, and Maria felt as though it had been the longest day of her life. She lay on the settee by the dying fire, and the incidents filled her mind in a positive kaleidoscope. Above all, one thing stood out. She had learned a lot about herself. There would be no going back to her old apathy. Whatever else happened in the next few days, something had been already successfully conquered, and the new knowledge about herself would remain. She didn't doubt that she and Brand would continue to strike the sparks off each other for as long as they remained at the house. That was as inevitable as night following day. They had both made an effort, but it hadn't been of much use. Their personalities were so diverse that civilised behaviour didn't stand a ghost of a chance of surviving for long.

She lay on her side and gazed into the grey and red ashes that glowed softly in the fireplace. A piece of coal moved, fell slightly, and a few sparks flared briefly before vanishing. The room was still warm. Upstairs, Brand was in bed, comfortable and, she hoped, fast asleep. Maria was exhausted, but knew there was no chance of sleep yet. The settee was hard and not quite long enough to be stretched out on. She wondered how Brand, with his greater height and weight, had ever managed to sleep the previous night, and eased herself up slightly to adjust her pillow before trying to settle down again.

She thought about what had happened so recently after their argument. She had gone in—after counting ten—and he had glared at her and asked what the hell she wanted.

'I heard a thud,' she said mildly. 'I thought you'd fallen.'

'I'd make a damned sight more noise than that if I fell,' he retorted.

'Then what *was* the noise?' She looked round the room. A book lay on the floor by the door and she went over to pick it up. 'Dear me, throwing books now? I used to do that too, when I was about five.' She gave him a sweet forgiving smile and put the book on the table.

She thought he muttered something but couldn't be sure. 'Did you speak?' she asked.

'Yes, but don't ask me to repeat it. You might not like it.'

'I'm quite sure I wouldn't,' she answered. 'You must know a lot of words I've never heard of. The kettle's nearly boiling, thank goodness. Then I can fill your hot water bottle—*again*——' that word was subtly emphasised, 'and you can go to beddy-byes. You should have brought your teddy bear with you. They're very good for flinging around in temper and they don't do much damage.' She walked out on that splendid exit line and ran up to get his bottle.

Now, remembering, she had to smile. She pulled the duvet more closely over her and tried to snuggle down. The calm, sweet Maria hadn't lasted long, but she didn't mind. With Brand, anything but red-blooded attack and defence was unthinkable. He was maddening—and stimulating. Her brain and mind were crystal-sharp with the sheer effort of holding her own in their running battle of words. One thing he would never be was dull. And life, for those around him, would never be dull either. She wondered if he had a girl-friend—or a mistress. She had been left in no doubt that he was a virile, sexually aggressive male, none at all. For the first time she allowed herself to think about what had happened—or rather, so nearly happened—when he had helped massage her.

He had despised himself, and almost certainly her, for the lack of self-control which had so nearly led to their making love. She knew now, with a deep sense of shame, that she would not have stopped him. She had wanted him, and still did, in a way she had never wanted any man. And he, at that time, had wanted her. It had been unspoken between them ever since, but it had in a way coloured their every action and reaction to each other. The sparks that they had triggered off, the smouldering and at times startling tension that filled them both when they were near each other—all these had their roots in the one incident. Maria moved restlessly, her body warm with the memories. They were disturbing to her. She wanted not to think about them, she shouldn't think about them. During the afternoon, when she had lain in bed with him, there had been a sweet aching inside her. He had been ill, and of course she was safe, but there had been a brief moment of fantasy, wondering what he would be like making love.

Her head throbbed dully with tension and she rubbed her neck slowly, remembering the sensuous touch of his hands, the gentle smooth touch that had caused the blurring of her senses. The kiss, and what had gone afterwards, had been quite inevitable.

She sat up, wide awake, heart pounding. It was no use; she would never sleep. She pattered out barefoot into the darkened kitchen and poured herself a small drop of whisky. There was no lamp lit, and it wasn't safe to make a hot drink in the dark. She stood there, her feet cold on the stone floor, and it had the effect of cooling her down both mentally and physically. She sipped the whisky and it was strong and effective. Putting the empty glass down, she was about to creep back when she heard a groan from upstairs. Her scalp prickled. She stood at the foot of the stairs and listened. Brand might have been dreaming, or turning over in his sleep. It wouldn't be repeated . . . But it was, moments later, this time louder. It was the sound of a man in pain.

She ran up the stairs and into the room, and said softly: 'Brand, are you all right?'

There was a startled movement, he turned, and winced. 'Maria? What is it?'

'I heard you—I thought you were in pain,' she said.

'It's my neck. You were right, it hurts like hell. I've been trying to get the pillow right.'

She bent over him. 'Here, let me.' She smoothed and adjusted the pillow. 'There, is that better?'

'Yes, thanks.' But she knew he didn't mean it.

'Move over a bit if you can. I'll sit on the bed and rub your neck.' She heard him moving, and sat down. The room was in pitch darkness, and very cold.

'Are you warm enough?' she asked.

'Yes, very warm. And you?'

'Never mind me.' She leaned over. 'Now, where does it hurt?'

'Just there—ouch! That's it——'

'I'll be gentle,' she soothed, and began rubbing carefully, gently. She was glad he wasn't a mind-reader. Her thoughts were more controlled now, but her heart was beating very rapidly.

'Mmm, that's better,' he said. 'You mustn't get cold, you know.'

'I know. I'll only do it for a few more minutes. You——' she stopped.

Oh, dear Lord, this was awful! She could feel the warmth of him, feel the hair that grew at the nape of his neck, beautiful dark hair. His neck was so strong and powerful . . . It would be better if she left now, for something was happening to them both, she knew it as well as she knew her own name. Electric tension, filling the air, almost tangible. Her hand faltered, he reached up and touched her face, and she heard his indrawn breath.

'Your cheeks are cold,' he said, and his voice had gone harsh, almost husky, very quiet.

'I'll be all——'· She didn't finish. He reached up both hands, pulled her down to him, and kissed her.

'Thank you,' he said a moment later. Maria pulled herself away.

'I'd better go,' she said. She could scarcely breathe for the pounding of her heart.

'You haven't finished my neck yet,' murmured Brand, and pulled aside the covers. 'Lie here where it's warm and do it.'

She knew that she shouldn't. She knew also that she was going to. She slid in next to him, and, still half sitting up, took hold of his neck again. His body was burning next to hers. The bed was truly wonderfully warm, and extremely comfortable. She was not going to stay longer than a few minutes more or she wouldn't be able to leave, she knew that.

'Ah——!' he cried out suddenly, and she stopped.

'What have I done?' she whispered.

'It hurt. It's all right, your hands are very gentle. It's not your fault——'

She began rubbing again, and somehow, she wasn't sure how it happened, she found herself sliding down a bit so that she was nearer. Whether he moved too she wasn't quite certain, but now their bodies were touching.

'I think,' she said slowly, 'I'd better go.'

'Yes,' he answered huskily, 'I suppose you better

had——' He stopped, and his hand slid round her back. 'Are you a little warmer?'

'I'm—too—warm,' she murmured. 'I'm——' She couldn't speak. She felt his warm hand caressing her back. He slid it under her sweater and gently massaged her spine.

'So you are,' he said, as if surprised. 'So you are.'

'Brand,' she said, after several moments of sheer blissful touch, 'I think you'd better stop right now.' She found it difficult to speak. He found it equally difficult to answer, that much was obvious as he removed his hand, trailing along her skin in a trail of fire.

'You'd better go now,' he whispered, 'or I'm not going to be responsible for my actions——' He moved slightly away, and his breathing was shallow and sharp. 'I had no right——'

She didn't move. 'For God's sake, go!' he muttered fiercely.

'It wasn't me who got into your bed uninvited,' she whispered. 'Is this what you intended?'

'I don't know. You were freezing, that was all I thought—at first—and then——' he stopped, and turned his head away.

Maria sat up, jerking the covers with her. 'I hate you sometimes,' she said, 'and I hate you now. Do you hear? I must have been mad to come up here—you really took me in with those groans——' she flung the covers to one side and a sheet caught her foot and she struggled to free it, but Brand turned and caught her wrist before she could slide out of the bed.

'Damn you!' he grated. 'That wasn't an act.'

'I don't think you know when you are acting,' she snapped, and tried to pull her hand free. 'Let me go— you told me to, and now you're stopping me!' She pulled in vain at his hand with her free one, and he sat up and jerked her towards him.

His mouth came down on hers with a savagery that frightened her. She was quite helpless, powerless to move. He might be ill, but he had lost none of his strength. He pulled her down so that she was beside him and then imprisoned her legs with one of his. Maria had a fleeting moment of panic at the sheer power of his attack—and then, to her dismay, found herself caught up in the sensuality of it all.

She cried out something, a wordless sound, and put her arms around his hard, lean, muscular body, revelling in the touch of him against her.

Brand's mouth was on her ear, kissing, whispering; she was aware of all vestiges of control slipping away from her as he caressed her with warm expert hands, leaving no doubt in her—not that there had ever been any—that he knew what he was doing. Then he paused—reluctantly, that was obvious. He lay very still, unmoving, hands resting on her thighs, and all she could hear was his fast shallow breathing. She found herself beginning to tremble helplessly. 'Brand——?' she whispered, questioning.

'This is madness,' he said thickly.

She already knew that, knew that it was one thing to fantasise, to imagine him making love, quite another to actually do it. Her senses reeled, but some vestiges of sanity remained, and she knew without a doubt that if she stayed there for much longer in his bed she would make love with him. 'Yes,' she whispered, 'I know.'

'Please go. If you don't, I will. I can't—stay like this much longer.'

He touched her face and felt the tears trickling down her cheeks, and she heard his indrawn breath. 'Has any man ever made love to you before?' he asked.

'No.'

He caught his breath. 'I thought not. I knew.'

She began to sob helplessly, relief mingling with regret, and he said: 'Please don't cry.'

'I—c-can't help it,' she whispered.

'Dear God!' his voice was agonised. 'You don't know what you're doing to me.' He put his hand to her cheek as if to quell the tears. 'Don't you understand what I'm saying? You must go—leave me now.'

'I'm—going.' Maria gave a long shuddering sigh. 'I'm so cold, so cold.'

'I daren't touch you. I wanted to make love to you, to possess you, because you made me so angry—but that's not the way it should be.' His voice was low, and he spoke quietly as if he had to say what he did before he could change his mind. 'That's how it was the other night—I knew what I was doing, what I intended, and then I couldn't go through with it. Now you know— and now we both know that we must leave here as soon as it's possible. I don't blame you for trying to get away as you did. My anger was with myself, not you. I wanted to beat you, when it was myself I despised.' His voice shook. 'The feelings we have are intense, I know that. I know too why you must leave the agency. I pretended not to, but I knew. It's better that we never see each other again when we leave here. There's something in us both—we would destroy each other eventually.' He took a deep breath, and he too was trembling.

'Yes, I know,' she said, and her heart ached because she loved him—but she knew it was absolutely true. It was impossible to be in love with someone and know that it was so wrong as to be madness. She lay back on the pillow because she was safe. They were only inches apart, but the gulf between them was as wide and deep as an ocean. 'I know how you make me feel. There's anger in us with each other and perhaps we'll never know why, only that it exists. Yes, we must leave soon. I tried earlier today, I thought about it a lot and tried to rationalise the feeling, and I decided that we must, for our own sakes, behave in a civilised way. I can tell you now, because it's not going to make any difference, that I wanted you to make love to me, and I've never wanted any man before, and I'm being honest with you for perhaps the first time. Our ways and our lives are different, we're worlds apart in everything, but I'd—I'd like you to know that I respect you for what you've told me.'

She turned her face into the pillow and let the tears flow freely at last. Brand put his hand gently on her shoulder.

'Weep if you must,' he said. 'Sometimes tears can chase sadness away.'

They neither of them moved or spoke, and gradually she was spent, tears all gone, and she lay there exhausted.

She was warm and comfortable, drained of all emotion, and she knew with a deep sure instinct that it was the same for him too. The tension, almost tangible before, had gone. They were both safe from the storm that had assailed them.

She heard his breathing, and it was steady and even now, as was hers. Her head began to swim, as though she were going to faint, but it was with sheer exhaustion, nothing more. She would go in a minute, she knew that, and Brand would not try to stop her. She closed her eyes. His hand rested, still on her shoulder, an impersonal touch, no more. Thoughts drifted, pictures came to her, some sharp, others blurred. The sooner they left the better it would be for both. That was her last coherent thought before she fell asleep.

When she awoke it was morning, and Brand was in the bed, and still asleep. The bed was six feet wide, and he

**Begin a long love affair** with **SUPERROMANCE**.
Accept *Love beyond Desire,* free. Mail the postage-paid card below, today.

### SUPERROMANCE
1440 South Priest Drive, Tempe, AZ 85281.

Mail this card today.

# FREE! Mail to: **SUPERROMANCE**
1440, South Priest Drive, Tempe, Arizona 85281

**YES,** please send me FREE and without any obligation, my **SUPERROMANCE** novel, *Love beyond Desire.* If you do not hear from me after I have examined my FREE book, please send me the 3 new **SUPERROMANCE** books every month as soon as they come off the press. I understand that I will be billed only $2.50 per book (total $7.50). There are no shipping and handling or any other hidden charges. There is no minimum number of books that I have to purchase. In fact, I may cancel this arrangement at any time. *Love beyond Desire* is mine to keep as a FREE gift, even if I do not buy any additional books.

CI021

| | |
|---|---|
| Name | (Please Print) |
| Address | Apt. No. |
| City | |
| State | Zip |

Signature    (If under 18, parent or guardian must sign.)

### SUPERROMANCE

*A compelling love story of mystery and intrigue… conflicts and jealousies… and a forbidden love that threatens to shatter the lives of all involved with the aristocratic Lopez family.*

Mail this card today for your FREE book.

lay a foot or so away, on his side, facing her. She had slept deeply and well, no nightmares, not even a dream that she could remember. She felt relaxed and better than she had since coming to the house. She watched Brand objectively for a few minutes, remembering the things he had said, things that were so true, that she had known but would not have been able to put into words. Again she had seen another side to this man. Truly he was apart from others by his very character. More powerful than she could have ever imagined, he had said things that a lesser man would not have dared. He was all the more strong for having said them. How she loved him, and the love was a sweet pain inside her. Her life would never be the same again, and she too was richer for having met him.

She slipped silently out of bed and went downstairs. It might even be possible to leave today. It would certainly be the best thing. It all depended on how fit Brand was. The mist, when she drew back the curtains, had lifted. The grass had a dull grey sheen to it, as though it still bore lingering traces of the damp, but the air was sharp and clear. Her first task was to fetch her case and bag, though heaven knew what state they would be in—or her car. She pulled a face. There was only one way to find out. She put on her coat and went out into the cold morning air.

The walk did her good. It was over rough hummocky ground, towards the sea, and she saw her car first, on its side being pounded by waves, and her heart sank. She went as near as she dared, to look at it. She had loved her little Mini, but one thing was sure: it would never be quite the same again. Maria suddenly realised that it didn't matter. It was an object, a possession, no more than that. There were far more important things in life. She turned and walked away from it and picked up her case and bag. Both were damp, but, she hoped, not so inside. She would find that out when she reached the house.

She set off walking back, and several gulls swooped overhead, silent and watchful, in case she had food. She was hungry too. There was a little bread left, and some marmalade, and enough milk for two cups of coffee.

Maria opened the front door, put the case and bag down and went out to fill the kettle before lighting the fire. It was slightly warmer inside than out, but not much. The sooner a roaring fire was going, the better.

She was busily employed in raking out the ashes when she heard Brand's voice and looked up to see him standing in the doorway. She smoothed her hair from her eyes. 'Good morning,' she said.

'Good morning.' He walked in. 'Did you—stay all night?'

'I'm afraid so,' she responded. 'I fell asleep after our—talk.'

'I thought I'd imagined it. I woke up in the night and saw you—then just now thought I'd been dreaming.'

'No, you weren't.' It was like talking to a stranger, casually, even though they were discussing having shared a bed. 'It won't happen again, of course. We might be able to leave today, if you feel better.'

'Much.'

'I'll have a look at your cut when I've done the fire. The dressing will need changing anyway.' She picked up the hot tray, overflowing with cinders and ashes.

'Can I take that out?' asked Brand.

'No, stay where you are. I won't be a minute. The wood's outside with the coal, isn't it?'

'Yes.' Brand sat down on the settee where she had intended to spend the night. So much for intentions, Maria thought as she went out.

They breakfasted on toast, marmalade and coffee, sitting to eat it by the fire, and they spoke of her work for his firm. It was as if, by mutual and unspoken consent, their conversations were going to be quite impersonal.

Afterwards she took the plaster off his forehead, bathed and cleaned the cut, and decided to leave it uncovered. 'You're the boss,' he said agreeably, as he sat in the kitchen watching her.

Maria smiled wryly but said nothing. 'We'll go and try and get your car out,' he went on. 'What was the water level when you went?'

'The car's half out, half in. About three feet deep at that point, I'd say,' she answered.

'Okay. I've got a tow rope in the back of the Rover. Can you drive one?'

'I never have, but I'll try.'

'Let's go,' he told her. 'We'll also get an idea of what time we can leave. Are you ready to go today?'

'Yes. If you are?'

'I feel fine. Give me a couple of hours, I'll know.'

They went out the back way, and he said: 'I'll let you drive to the beach. Get in.'

Maria studied the gears for a moment or two, waited until he was seated, and switched on. The size of the vehicle was the first shock, and the steering was far harder, but Maria was quick to learn, and by the time they reached the beach, felt confident of being able to control the Land Rover in the tricky operation of pulling her car out of the water.

Brand wore a pair of waders that he had found at the house, and he attached the tow rope to the back of the Land Rover. Maria had driven it as near to the water as was safely possible, and her Mini lay only feet away.

She watched Brand wading into the water, shouted:

'Good luck,' and stood poised for him to tell her when to drive forward. He bent, jacketless, pullover sleeves rolled as far up as they would go, and fumbled under the water for the bumper of the Mini. After a few minutes he straightened up.

'Drive very slowly,' he shouted, 'and no more than four yards forward. Understand?'

'Yes,' she called. 'Got it!'

She adjusted the rear view mirror to see him clearly, started up, and inched forward. She put the brakes on the second he shouted to her, and jumped out.

Her Mini was upright, still in the water, a sorry, seaweed-covered sight. Maria should have felt like crying, but she wanted to laugh instead. She didn't care!

'Okay. Now, forward again, a few more yards.'

He stood beside it, leaning in through the open driver's window, one hand on the steering wheel, the other on the side.

Maria obeyed, slowly, slowly, steadily, two yards, four yards, slower, then stopped. Her car was on solid ground again, looking very dejected.

Brand came over to her. 'Okay, your work's done. I'll leave it here, and when we go, I'll tow it to the village. There's a garage there—of sorts—and we'll have to leave it.'

'I understand,' she nodded.

He looked at it. 'It's a mess, isn't it?' It was a rhetorical question. 'I haven't a clue how much it'll cost to put right.'

'It doesn't matter,' she answered.

He looked at her sharply as they got in the Land Rover, he in the driver's seat now. 'You said that as though you meant it.'

'I did.' She glanced sideways at him. 'You don't have to look at me as though I'm crazy. That's just the way I feel today.'

'Because we're leaving?'

'Possibly. Things have changed, that's the only way I can put it.'

'You know, you're quite a remarkable woman.' And he started up the engine before she could reply, if indeed she could have thought of any way to respond.

When they reached the house Brand parked the Land Rover in front of it with the keys inside. Whistling, he jumped down and walked round to Maria's side. The door had stuck, and he opened it for her and held out his hand for her to take. She hesitated momentarily, then held it and jumped down. 'Thanks.'

'We'd better do any final clearing up now, pack up, and be ready to leave,' he told her. 'The causeway should be clear early afternoon. Agreed?'

'Yes, you're right. I'll throw out all the food that's left just before we go.' Maria pushed open the front door and warm air enfolded them. It was like coming home. Home.

'Some fire you made. It will be a shame to let that go down,' he remarked.

'Yes.' She went over, knelt and poked it, sending a shower of sparks upward. She knew quite suddenly that she didn't want to leave. She wanted to stay with Brand here and be with him and love him . . .

'I'll make us both a coffee,' he told her, and went to the kitchen. Maria sat back on the carpet and looked round the room. It was still early, barely ten, and they would leave about three, no later. Five hours alone and then back to civilisation. And during the five hours there would be surface talk, there would be nothing serious because there was nothing could be added to what had taken place during the night. There was a mental drawing away, each from the other, Maria sensed it. Each separate, and in a way alone. They had come closer to understanding each other during their conversation in bed than at any other time. But that was over and done with.

Maria's new life was ahead, waiting for her in London. She stood up. She had to check every drawer and cupboard in the house before they went, to make sure that nothing was left behind. And in a few days, Rhu-na-Bidh, the House of the Elms, would be just a memory.

It was growing dark as they reached the borders of Scotland and England. Brand had already switched on the headlights and they travelled down the main road at a good speed. Little had been said on the long journey from the island. Maria was engrossed in her thoughts, thinking ahead, and he was apparently concentrating on driving on the roads which were treacherous with rain.

They had already decided that they would have to stop for the night somewhere en route, and when Brand suggested Kendal as being a good halfway point, she had agreed. She had committed herself to leaving her job, and it would be impossible for her to stay, but she was faintly worried about finding other work. She had a moderate legacy from her father, but had decided never to touch it, except in dire emergency.

She had savings too, enough to live on for a while if nothing turned up, and she had a married cousin, Janice, who ran a busy hotel near Cambridge with her husband, and who would welcome Maria's help at any time.

She just wished she had more time to look around before leaving. The man responsible for her decision spoke.

'Hungry? Want to stop for a meal yet?'

'Not particularly. Are you?'

'I will be soon. It will do us good anyway. We'll go another fifty or sixty miles and then see. Will you look in the guide?'

'Yes, of course.' There was a small map light and she studied both map and food guide to find somewhere to eat. 'There's a place called the Ship Inn about seventy miles on. Recommended for its steaks.'

'Sounds fair enough. Let me know well before we turn off.'

Maria sat back. The Land Rover was more comfortable than she had imagined it would be. They would sleep at a hotel, leave early, and arrive in London at noon the next day. And there she would say goodbye to Brand. She was due in at the agency on Wednesday, and at the weekend she might visit Janice. She badly needed someone to talk to. She couldn't tell Janice the circumstances of meeting Brand, but she desperately wanted to tell her about him. If she hadn't met him, she wouldn't be leaving, but she had, and although there were things to regret, there was so much more to treasure, to remember, to store away in a secret part of her mind and bring out from time to time.

She wondered if she would ever again meet a man like him. There would be other men in her life, there always had been, and there was Tony. She thought of him guiltily. She had practically forgotten his existence for the past couple of days, giving him scarcely a thought.

She knew she was going to finish with him; it would be unfair to do otherwise. She sighed.

'Tired?' asked Brand.

'No. Just—thinking. I'm getting hungry, as a matter of fact.'

'Good. We'll soon be there.' He spared her a brief glance. 'We still haven't sorted out the matter of the house.'

'I thought we had.'

'No. We ought to meet soon and decide finally.'

That would be dangerous. The break must be soon, and it must be clean, which was the reason she was leaving Prothero and Michaels.

'Can we talk about it in the morning?' she asked.

'Will you have decided then?'

'I don't know.' She looked out at the darkened countryside. She had only to say, 'I love you' and he'd run a mile. He wouldn't want to see her. He didn't know what love was. But those were three words that could never be said. Not to him. Not ever.

# CHAPTER SEVEN

EACH mile that passed was a mile nearer parting. Maria's throat was dry, and there was a dull pain in the region of her heart. It was nine in the morning. Soon they would be in London, in less than three hours.

They had stayed in a hotel near Kendal the previous night, after dining well at the restaurant she had discovered. Brand had been polite and courteous, and like a stranger. She knew that he would be relieved when they said goodbye. It was obvious he wanted to forget the cottage and all its associations, and she, remembering his shock of discovery about his mother, knew why.

'Have you thought about the cottage?' he asked, after a long silence during which she had watched passing cars on the motorway and tried to think about what would happen soon.

'Yes. I don't want it. Please, let's leave things as they are, shall we?'

'Legally mine?'

'Yes. I don't want——' she faltered, 'anything.'

His face was cold and hard. 'If that's what you've decided, so be it.'

'It is.'

'Where do you live?' he asked.

'In Hampstead. You can drop me anywhere. I'll get a taxi.'

'Don't be ridiculous. I'll take you home.'

'But I don't——' she stopped.

'Don't want me to know where you live? That's

rather stupid. *If* I wanted to find out I could do so easily from the agency.' His tone was dismissive. 'I shall merely drop you off. I don't want to come in, you needn't worry.'

Maria felt herself flush at the bleak words. Brand made himself quite clear. She was being stupid to even imagine he would want to.

'Then thank you, I'll appreciate that.'

There was a silence again. They stopped soon afterwards at a motorway service station for petrol, and had coffee, but as they neared home Brand became even more of a stranger. What else could she expect? After their brief shared intimacy he would regret even more than she his unburdening of himself. She had sensed that he was a very private man, probably a loner, a man who walked alone through the world, needing no one, confiding in few, if any. Complex and fascinating and attractive, yes, all those, but not actually *needing* anyone.

He drove through the sprawling outskirts of northern London at just past one, and said: 'You'd better give me directions.'

'Yes. Keep on this road for about three miles, then it's a left turn—I'll direct you again then.'

The traffic was heavy and conversation would have been difficult even if they had wanted to talk—which neither did. The familiar landmarks came into sight. Maria's heart ached. 'Left here,' she said quietly. 'To the end and right.'

Ten minutes later Brand drew up at the end of her road. The huge Victorian houses were well kept, with small gardens front and rear. It was a quiet road, practically every house converted into flats, and mainly let to business people, artists, radio and T.V. backroom workers, a hotch-potch of the creative ones of the world. Maria had been lucky to get herself a large rambling flat on the first floor of one of the houses, and enjoyed living there.

'How far down?' he asked.

'Here will do fine,' she answered, trying to sound bright, covering up the dark heavy lump that had lodged in her stomach.

'How far, I said?'

'Half way, on the left, number fifty-four.'

'Right.' He cruised slowly along and stopped. Maria had forgotten about her door sticking and had to wait for him to open it. He brought her case round with him and put it on the pavement.

For a few moments they stood facing each other, then Maria broke the silence. 'Thank you for running me all the way home. Goodbye, Brand.'

It seemed for just a second, as though he was about to say something. Then a pause, and: 'Goodbye, Maria.'

He turned and walked away, round the front of the Land Rover. Maria picked up the suitcase and walked across the pavement to the gate. She didn't look back, not even when she heard the engine roar into life. As she opened the gate he drove away. The noise faded. She turned round and looked along the road to see him turning a corner, and the next second he had gone.

A kind of silence filled her. The street wasn't all that quiet. Cars passed in the distance, there was the constant faint hum of even more far away traffic, but it was nothing to her because Brand had gone. It was more than an inner silence, it was an emptiness.

Maria opened the door and went upstairs, suddenly weary. There was a flash of movement, blurred, a loud purring sound, and she was nearly tripped up by a large white cat which was trying to twine its body round her ankles.

'Cleo!' she exclaimed, and began to laugh, sadness temporarily forgotten. She bent to scoop the animal up under her free arm and continued climbing the stairs with the purring bundle trying to lick her chin. 'You idiot,' she said softly, still laughing, and a voice floated down from the second floor:

'Hi! Saw you arrive. Got time to come up for a drink?'

'I'd love to, Cassie. Just give me five minutes to wash. Did you send Cleo down?' Maria looked upwards. A tall kaftaned woman with waist-length hair was leaning over the banister rail.

'Yes. She started scratching the door five minutes ago. Saw you arrive, my sweet. My, that was some *dishy* man! I expect to hear *all*!' her head vanished, only the echo of her rich throaty laugh remaining, and Maria reached her door, put cat and case down, opened it and went in. The flat smelt faintly musty and she opened the window and went into the bathroom to wash. She now had mixed feelings about having accepted Cassandra's invitation so readily. No way would she be able to prevaricate with the woman who lived in the flat above. Bright, bubbly, a larger than life personality in every way, Cassandra Farr, alias Cassie, talented illustrator of picture stories in teenage magazines, was not a person to be fooled by anybody.

Maria sighed, picked up Cleo, locked her door and ran up. The door was wide open, the large front room a litter of posters, scatter cushions and bright rugs. Practically every available surface was covered with paper, blank, sketched in, or coloured. Cassandra emerged from her kitchen, pushing the huge granny glasses she wore more firmly on.

'Kettle's on,' she beamed. 'I'd offer you wine, but I've just run out, so it'll have to be coffee. Find your-

self a chair, love, and park yourself. God, those cats!'
She swept a tattered cushion on to the floor. A few
feathers floated downwards with it, and Cleo jumped
from Maria's arms and took a flying leap at them. 'See
what I mean? Little devils think the damned cushion's
a scratching post. So, how are you, what's new, and
*who* was that beautiful guy?' She hadn't paused for
breath since coming in, but now she did, waiting expectantly for an answer.

Maria was fond of Cassie. They had known each
other for more than two years, and while Cassie was a
bubbling extrovert with dozens of friends of either
sex, parties every week, boundless energy and enthusiasm, she was also discreet and trustworthy. Maria had
no intention of telling her more than a few details
about Brand, because it was too secret and precious
ever to be told—but at the same time she knew with a
kind of dazed awareness that Cassie had her own
subtle ways of finding out anything she wanted to
know, or rather, what she thought she needed to know
so that she could help and advise. She was, as well as
being an extrovert, a great solver of everyone's problems.

There was no possible way she would solve this one,
thought Maria wryly, but one thing was, she wouldn't
be able to sit and brood about anything in her flat.

She accepted an elaborately patterned bowl of
coffee. Not for Cassie ordinary cups and beakers.
'Drink. Want anything to eat as well?'

Maria shook her head. 'No, thanks, this is fine.
Listen, if you're busy I won't stay long——'

'I'm always busy, but we can talk while I draw. So,
what's new—and who is he, for God's sake? I don't
blame you for wanting to keep him under wraps, but
we are friends, you know. I have a *right*——'

'His name's Brand Cordell and I met him about

three days ago and he dropped me off at my flat—as you saw—and that's *it*!'

Wide-eyed, her spectacles on the end of her nose, Cassie pulled up a beanbag cushion and sat crossed-legged on it facing Maria.

'That's *it*?' she squealed. 'You expect me to accept *that*?'

Maria nodded. 'Please. For now.'

'Oh, oh,' Cassie nodded wisely. 'The big one—too secret and wonderful to talk about. Right?' She was teasing, but unfortunately her teasing was too near to the truth, and Maria felt her face tighten with the effort at control. Cassie's eyes softened. She saw. She *was* far too shrewd. 'Oh, Maria, I'm sorry. Me and my big mouth! Tell me to mind my own business. I deserve it.'

Maria moved the bowl round in her hands. 'I—I can't——' She began, and bit her lip. 'Oh, *hell*, what's the use? I've fallen for him. Stupid, silly me has to go and fall for someone I'm never going to see again.' She looked up, face anguished. 'Now you know.'

'I won't say another word. Promise.' Cassie gave a Scout salute so solemnly that Maria had to smile.

'It's not that I don't want to tell you, I can't talk about him—not yet anyway.'

'Fair enough. Now, let's see, what *shall* we talk about? I'm having a few friends round tonight. You're invited. It'll do you good. How about it?'

Maria shook her head. 'Thanks, but I'll leave it. Perhaps the next time?'

'Okay.' Cassie nodded. 'As long as you don't mind if there's a bit of noise.'

'I'll put my ear plugs in. Thanks for the warning,' Maria laughed.

'That's better. I thought you'd forgotten how.' Cassie sighed. 'Phew! You do look a bit tired, if you don't mind me saying so. Why don't you go down now, curl up for an hour or two? I'll creep round like a little mouse, honest—and I'll pop down about six and see how you are. Okay?'

'You're a pal.' Maria finished her coffee and stood up. 'I think I'll do just that. Thanks for the drink.'

'See you later, then?'

'Yes, later. 'Bye for now.' Maria deposited Cleo on her chair and went, leaving a thoughtful Cassie finishing her own coffee. Within minutes she was fast asleep on the settee in her own flat.

The week passed, and it had an unusual quality to it. Maria did her shopping, her normal tasks, and she went to work, knowing that on the Monday of the week following she would be handing in her resignation. It was with a sense of relief that she came home on the Friday evening after a hectic day, and had a hot relaxing bath. She was going to spend the evening alone by a warm fire—electric, not a wild glorious coal one as had been at Rhu-na-Bidh—and watch television and not allow herself to *think*.

Tony was away, and she hadn't seen him all week. He had had a call from his mother in Oxford to say that his father was ill, and had telephoned Maria twice during the week. She, knowing that she certainly couldn't tell him anything shattering on the phone, had wisely said nothing, being concerned only with his and his parents' wellbeing. She came off the phone feeling wretched both times, but there was nothing she could do about that. He hadn't sensed anything different in her manner, being too worried about his own problems, and that was in a way a relief.

Now, Friday evening, and Maria sitting by the fire with bank statements was going over her finances and discovering to her surprise that she had more money than she remembered. She certainly had enough to live on, with her own personal savings, because she had always been thrifty, and the interest from the money left her by her father, if necessary for a year or more. It was a comforting and reassuring thought.

She finished totting up a column of figures and rubbed her eyes wearily. She had a slight headache, but apart from that was feeling better than she had for days. Memories of Brand were strong. He intruded in her dreams every night, and his was the face she saw in her mind's eye on waking each morning. It wasn't the faintest good even trying to forget him yet. She had been very conscious of him when she had gone into work on the Wednesday. He was her employer, indirectly, and she was certainly the only one who had ever met him—apart from, perhaps, her immediate boss, the manager of the agency, Mike Grahame, a tough, hard-drinking, chain-smoking man who was respected and well liked by the staff. Respected because he was ruthless and a shrewd arranger, who wined and dined clients and stole accounts from under other agencies' noses, who had a certain rough charm that appealed to men as well as women and allowed him to get away with murder on occasions, and liked because he was strictly fair and would defend the staff all the way in the rare event of a dissatisfied advertiser grumbling. Maria didn't want to leave, and giving in her notice wasn't going to be easy. She might possibly have to tell him her main reason—although with as few details as possible—for she could also trust him to keep his own counsel in the matter.

She sighed and began to fold all her papers back into the box file she kept them in. Nearly ten. She was going up to Cassie's the following evening, and on Sunday visiting Janice and Tom. On Sunday evening she was going to write her notice out. That would not be easy . . .

Nor was it easy on Monday morning, when, carrying two cups of coffee, she went into Mike Grahame's office at eleven and said: 'Mike, can I see you?'

He sat back in his chair and looked hard at her. Flaming red hair, cigar permanently at the corner of his mouth, bright blue eyes, cleft in his chin, he was irreverently called, 'the Leprechaun' by all who worked for him. But only behind his back.

'You know something,' he said, 'I wondered when you'd be in to see me. Sit down. Thanks for the coffee, and tell me why you've come.'

His eyes were too shrewd. 'You wondered when I'd be in?' she said, puzzled. 'I don't understand.'

'You will, honey, you will.' He ground out the cigar and began to pat his pockets for matches. 'Blast it, where are——'

'On your desk.' She handed him the box and he took it with a grunt.

The performance of lighting his cigar took a few moments and Maria knew enough not to speak during it. Mike puffed contentedly, blew a smoke ring into the air and said: 'Right, let's hear it.'

'I've come to hand in my resignation, Mike——' she began, and he said:

'I know bloody well you have, and I've never heard such flaming rubbish in all my life.' He banged the desk with his fist and glared at her. 'So you can just go and set a match to it, or tear it into little pieces, and you can be thankful I'm too much of a gentleman to offer any other alternatives——'

'How did you know?' she gasped.

'How the hell did I know? How the hell do you *think* I knew?' he shouted. 'Because I had a meeting with Mr Cordell over the weekend, *that's* how I know!'

Maria, totally bereft of speech, could only sit and look at him dazedly. He clicked his fingers. 'Give it to me.' When she didn't move, he said it louder, making her jump.

She handed the sealed envelope to him and he glanced briefly at his name on it, then tore it in half with a grandiose flourish and dropped the two pieces in his waste paper basket. 'Now get back to work and don't let me hear any nonsense or I'll fire you!' he growled, then burst out laughing. 'Fire you! Get it?'

She stared stony-faced at him, white and shaking. He leaned both hands on the desk and stared across at her. 'Well? Lost your tongue?'

'You saw Brand Cordell?' she whispered.

'Well, I wouldn't know about his first name. To me he's *Mr* Cordell, if you get me. And yes, I did. I went to his house, at his invitation, and was wined and dined—and I do mean wined, only it was followed by neat whiskies after a while and I have a healthy respect for any man who can drink yours truly under the table, and he can, believe me, which is why I'm feeling extremely fragile this morning, and totally disenchanted with any bloody excuses you might care to give me—do I make myself clear?' He glared at her, then clutched his head. 'Go and get me some Alka-Seltzer, there's a good girl.' When she didn't move, he added: 'Now!' and she fled.

She gave him the fizzing glass and watched him drink the contents in one long swallow. He banged the glass on the desk and burped.

' 'Scuse me. That's a bit better. Now let's hear your version.'

'What did he tell you?' Maria didn't really believe this was happening. It couldn't be, could it? She was still dreaming.

' 'S'truth. Never mind what he told me. I want to know your reasons first, then I'll see which I believe.'

'I—I met him in Scotland, and we—er—didn't get

on very well—then I found out he owned the company and I realised I couldn't go on working here, not knowing I mean, only—well——' she faltered.

'Hell's bells! It's a good job you're more lucid at writing advertising blurbs than you are at talking or we'd have no bloody accounts left——'

'Stop it, Mike!' she cried, in desperation, and had the feeling—almost of satisfaction if she had been in any condition to appreciate it—of seeing him temporarily silenced. She put her hand to her mouth, horrified. No one in history had ever told Mike to be quiet. She wondered, almost impersonally, if he would sack her for insubordination. She had her second surprise of the morning a moment later. He pulled a face.

'Sorry, love,' he said. 'Here, drink your coffee.'

She swallowed. Mike had apologised? That wasn't possible either. She picked up her cup and drank. 'Now,' he said, and all the fire had gone from his voice, 'let's talk, nicely and sensibly, and let me tell you how much I value you working here—which I might not have told you too often, but when it comes to the crunch, like this, and I discover I might be about to lose you, I suddenly realise how much I don't want you to go. Repeat—don't want you to go.'

Maria sniffed as tears came to her eyes. 'Oh, Mike,' she said softly.

He cleared his throat. 'Don't turn on the taps, for God's sake. I've got the mother and father of a hangover, thanks to you—well, *partly* thanks to you,' he amended, as if trying to be strictly fair, 'and if you make me feel guilty about bullying you into crying I'll probably go to pieces and have to be carried out—so *please* stop.'

She took her handkerchief from her bag and blew her nose. 'That's better,' he said in relieved tones. 'Anyway, what on earth were you crying for? I was praising you, for God's sake. Would you feel better if I insulted you?'

She took her head. She even managed a little smile. 'No. Thank you, of course you were. I'm overwhelmed. And—very bewildered, I'm afraid.'

'Hmm, so was I. When he started on about you, I mean. How do you think I felt? Here's me, summoned for dinner—a kind of royal invitation, you might say—to our new lord and master, and he gives me all the old flannel about we're doing a great job, he's been studying the figures and we're keeping nicely afloat—and then he asks me questions about the accounts that prove to me he's a man who knows exactly what he's talking about, no fooling him, I can tell you, and we get into a deep discussion about business tactics during which he manages to hint very delicately that as far as he's concerned I'm doing a great job and he respects my judgment—and by this time the dinner's over and we're on the hard stuff, and I'm thinking what a hell of a fellow he is, and the whole world is a very mellow place.' He paused to drink his lukewarm coffee and winced.

'And then he asks me about the staff, and I tell him. We're practically bosom chums by now, and he'd got some King Edwards, and the air was blue with smoke and the bottle of whisky seems to be one of those that lasts for ever because, damn me, my glass was never empty, and I was beginning to think he was the greatest guy I'd ever met——' Mike stopped. 'Are you ready?'

Maria nodded. 'I think so. I'm not sure what for, though.'

He grinned. 'I'll tell you, honey. I'd already told him about you, being something special, I mean, and looking back I'll swear he didn't bat an eyelid at the time, but then he said, quite casually: "I've met Maria already. She hasn't given in her notice yet, then?"

'I must have stared at him as though he'd gone mad, because he nodded. "I'm afraid she might be going to," he said, and *I* said: "Look, I know Maria—I'd know if she wasn't happy, I assure you," and *he* said: "She was—until she found out I owned the firm," and *I* said: "I'm sorry, but I don't quite get you." Then he poured me out another glass of whisky from this enormous bottle and said something to the effect—and I wasn't taking in anything too well at that time, if you get me—that you and he had discovered you clashed and that *you'd* said you couldn't go on working here because as far as you were concerned he was "persona non grata" or to put it in my words, honey, I gathered you couldn't stand the sight of each other and you'd more or less told him he could go jump in the lake. Do I make myself clear, or have I been talking nonsense for the last five minutes?'

'You've made yourself perfectly clear, and you've about summed it up, Mike,' she said.

'Hmm. Well, I remember telling him like hell you were leaving, over my dead body I seem to recall saying, and I *seem* to remember him clapping me on the shoulder and topping up my glass and saying something to the effect that he'd known all along he could rely on me and we'd have to meet again soon and see about an adjustment of my salary.' He frowned. 'I don't remember too much after that, except that he put me in a car and had me driven home.' He clasped his hands and laid them on his desk. 'And now, my dear girl, I think you will understand precisely why I tore up your resignation. As I see it—and correct me if you think I'm wrong—I'm the blue-eyed boy who's going to get a nice raise in the near future—and somehow, although I'm not even sure how he managed to convey it to me, I know that if I let you leave, that raise will somehow get "forgotten".' He grinned in a fatherly fashion. 'Get it?'

'Only too well,' she said dryly.

'And incidentally,' he added, 'I did gather, during the course of the evening, that he has no intention of coming in and interfering. That seemed to be quite an important point.'

'All right, you win—or rather, he does. Though I don't see *why*,' she said. 'He told you himself we didn't get on, and it's perfectly true. We clashed like mad from the word go.'

'Funny world, ain't it,' agreed Mike equably. 'He's a business man, first and foremost. He made damned sure he had an unbiased opinion about your work *before* he told me. You make money for him—you stay, ducky, it's that simple. So.' He looked down at the two pieces of envelope in his bin. 'I did the right thing. Back you go to work. Can't sit here talking all day. Take the coffee cups with you.' He gave her a wolfish grin. 'Don't let it go to your head.'

Maria stood up. 'With you? No fear!' She was on her way to the door, holding the empty cups, when Mike's voice halted her.

'Hey——'

Maria turned. 'Yes?'

'You don't think——' he shrugged and pulled a face. 'Naw——'

'What?' she demanded.

'Does he fancy you?'

That hurt, it really did, though Mike hadn't intended it to. She managed a little smile. 'Heavens, no! What makes you say a thing like that?'

'It's funny——' he fumbled for his matches again. 'I mean, you'd think, you clashing like that an' all, he'd be glad for you to go, and—you are a good-looking wench, you know.'

'Thanks. Don't let your wife hear you!'

'Oh, she's broad-minded!' He laughed. 'You sure?'

'Sure what? That your wife's broad-minded?'

'No. That he doesn't fancy you.'

'Quite sure,' she said dismissively, and reached for the door handle.

'Hey, do *you*?' he said, more softly.

Maria froze. She couldn't turn round. '*No!*' she answered, and opened the door. It slammed behind her, she couldn't help it, someone had opened a window, and a draught caught it, but she suspected she heard a faint whistle as she walked away down the corridor.

She was greeted by leering winks and nudges when she went into the 'think tank' as the main office was called.

'Been having a cosy chat with Mike, eh?' Terry called from the paper-littered table he spent his days at, and Harry Morgan, a great tease, answered:

'Can't you see she's blushing? Leave her alone. Never mind him, Maria love, come and tell your Uncle Harry all about it. What did he want?'

She tossed her hair back. 'Wouldn't you love to know?' she said mysteriously. She went over to Harry's desk and looked severely at the sketch of a half-naked woman on it.

'Tut, tut, is that the best you can do?' She shook her head, as if sad, and he snatched the sketch away and pulled out his tongue at her.

'Go and see what's waiting on *your* desk—that'll wipe the smile off your face.' He patted her bottom as she went past him, and she aimed a half-hearted slap in the general direction of his arm, and laughed. The subject had been deflected from her interview with Mike, which was what she had intended. He would never mention anything about it to the others, she knew that.

She needed time to think about what had been said,

and the atmosphere in the office wasn't conducive to any private thought. People were constantly in and out, or would be shortly, and the place usually became a hive of activity by noon. It seemed better that she should concentrate on the various items lying on her desk for now and forget her puzzlement for the present. And this she was able to do.

Mike appeared briefly in the main office before going out to lunch with a prospective client, had a few words with Terry, Harry, and the others before coming over to where Maria sat deep in thought, designing a layout for a new advertisement. She wasn't even aware of his presence until he rapped on her desk with his knuckles. She looked up blankly, dragged away from composing a catchy jingle that was coming out nicely on paper.

'Okay?' he asked, and they both knew he wasn't referring to pizzas or any of the other things that littered her desk.

'Yes, fine.' She smiled up at him. 'Still suffering slightly from shock, but just fine.'

'Good.' He removed the cigar from his mouth and studied it for a moment. 'He telephoned me just now, and I told him you were staying. See you folks later,' he added more loudly as he turned away. 'Keep at it or I'll want to know why.' He was walking away. Maria wanted to ask him what Brand had said but knew Mike had timed his words deliberately so that it was impossible.

She watched him stroll out of the office, her face stunned. Brand had telephoned, here, to ask about her. She wondered what his motives were, and found her heart thudding. Why? Why on earth should he care whether she stayed or went? Except, as Mike had so shrewdly observed, Brand was a business man, first and foremost.

# CHAPTER EIGHT

BECAUSE Cassie had known that Maria intended giving in her notice, it was only fair to tell her that she had withdrawn it, and somehow, over glasses of cool white wine in Cassie's flat that evening, in that wonderfully warm, relaxed atmosphere, Maria discovered that she was telling the other woman far more of the story than she had intended.

Cassie listened. She was a good listener, who interjected only the occasional, 'Go on, how fascinating,' as she sat wide-eyed on her beanbag chair and plied Maria with more wine. The three cats, Peregrine, Orlando and Cleopatra, sprawled around in various stages of sleep on cushions, and Maria found her head beginning to swim with the effects of the wine and the warmth.

There was a pause after Maria finished, then Cassie said: 'And you're quite happy about staying?'

'I never really wanted to leave,' she admitted. 'I felt I had to, don't you see?'

'Frankly, no,' said Cassie. 'If you want my honest opinion, I don't see. Why the hell should it matter if he does own the firm? There's something that doesn't quite tie up. Either you've not told me the full story, or you need your head examining.'

'Thanks,' Maria acknowledged with a wry smile. 'Friends like you are a great comfort!'

'Come off it, love. You asked me. There *is* more, isn't there?'

Maria nodded. 'Yes. But I can't—talk about it.'

'Did he make love to you? Is *that* it?'

'No, he didn't. It's not that—it's the reason why we met I've not told you.' She sighed. 'It's very personal and it involves someone who's—dead.'

'Oh, my God! I'm sorry. It—was it your father?'

Maria nodded. 'Yes.'

'Look, don't tell me. I shouldn't pry, I know. But I knew there was something. He—Brand, that is—hurt you, didn't he?'

'Yes, very much.'

'But you still love him?'

'I didn't say that!' Maria gasped. 'What makes you say——'

'Come on, love, I'm older than you are, and I've seen a bit more of the world, and I *know*. You *are* in love with him, aren't you?'

'Yes.' Maria put her hand to her eyes. 'Oh, damn! M-men. They're not worth the trouble.'

'I know. I've been saying that for years!' said Cassie. 'But I still make mistakes. What about Tony? You've not even mentioned him.'

'He's nice, I'm very fond of him, but we're not for each other. I don't want to hurt him, but I'm going to have to. Better now than later. I'll forget Brand in a while, I'm sure, I'll meet other men, when I'm mentally free, and then,' she shrugged, 'we'll see.'

'Hmm. Course you will. You're young, you've got more personality in you than most people, you're very attractive, and you've got a super job. You don't know when you're well off. As for *him*—just accept the fact that you got your fingers burned. No lasting damage done. Put it down to the big E—experience.'

'You make me feel much better,' Maria admitted.

'What are friends for? Now I vote we stop talking about him and change the subject. Have a drop more of this disgusting plonk and I'll tell *you* all about what the Incredible Hulk said to me the other day when I went into the office to have lunch with him. They're bringing out a new pre-teenage picture mag, and he wants me to have a meeting with one of the directors to discuss policy. *Moi!*' Cassie began to laugh. And Maria listened, fascinated ...

Two days later, she saw Brand. She was making her way back to the office at the end of her lunch break, passing Fortnum and Masons, when she saw the familiar figure of the man who was never far from her thoughts step out on to the pavement. She faltered in her stride. Another minute and she would have almost collided with him. He stood alone, looking out towards the roadway, then lifted his arm. Maria's heart thudded. For a moment it seemed as though he looked in her direction ...

Riveted to the spot, she took in every inch of his appearance to store away. There could hardly have been a greater contrast in the man with whom she had spent several tension-loaded days, and the one who stood on the pavement now. He wore a suit that must have cost hundreds of pounds, absolutely immaculate, in a dark grey, and with a dazzling, white shirt and dark grey tie. He was superbly attractive, tall, magnificently built, his hair and face a study in smooth, hard, sophistication. This man was a world apart from the one she had thought she had known. She suddenly realised something that had been in her subconscious mind all along. He was no ordinary businessman, he was no ordinary man at all, he had the casual confident manner that only comes with inborn breeding. And she had dared to imagine herself in love with him! She shivered at the thought—and saw a black Daimler purr to the kerb and stop in front of him. As he opened the door, a woman clutching several Fortnum and Mason bags came out, and he turned impatiently

as if waiting for her, said something to which she gave
a laughing retort, and helped her in the car.

Maria's throat was dry. As she began to walk forward, Brand half turned, and for a split second their
eyes met. The next moment he was in the car, and it
glided away into the stream of traffic and disappeared.
She couldn't walk on yet. She turned to look into the
nearest window and it was full of gift hampers and
brightly decorated luxury foodstuffs. She saw nothing
of these, only the image of a woman she had seen for
just a few moments. A tall, striking-looking redhead
whose hair had been swept back and up in a chignon,
wearing a mink coat and high-heeled shoes. A picture
of striking elegance. Laughing, being waited for by
Brand, helped into a car by him. Very much together.

To see him alone had been almost a physical shock;
to see him with the woman had been doubly so. Maria
walked on hurriedly, mind in a turmoil of confused
images, seeing him as he had been, warm, touching,
holding her, wanting her—fighting her, snarling his
hurt and pain of discovery; cycling on a battered old
bike to the village; allowing her to nurse and comfort
him—all blurred and jumbled in a huge kaleidoscope
of fragmented memories. And then seeing him now
standing outside a luxury store, signalling to his car to
come and fetch him. The two images were almost irre-
concilable. No Land Rover, but a Daimler, shiny black
and new. No casual sweater and jeans but a beautifully
cut suit with waistcoat. Not a man on his own, the
loner she had thought him to be, but with a woman
who would manage to turn men's heads wherever she
went. The kind of woman who was interviewed in the
glossy magazines, photographed in an elegant mansion.

The pain was sharp, and Maria recognised it. Sheer

blinding jealousy. She hurried on, scarcely aware of people passing, barely noticing the traffic until a man grabbed her arm as she was about to cross a road and said, in broad Cockney: 'Watch it, ducks!' as she saw the lorry that would have undoubtedly hit her go past.

'Thanks. I'm sorry,' she gasped, shaken, and he wagged a warning finger and grinned at her as he strode away. It had the effect of bringing her sharply back to reality. And when she reached the office she plunged into work as though her life depended on it, and decided that it had been the best thing that could have happened, seeing Brand like that. Now perhaps she could begin to forget him. Perhaps . . .

She succeeded. At least, she convinced herself that she had succeeded, which, although not quite the same thing, was nearly as good. Ideas poured from her, she stayed overtime several evenings, saw friends on others, went to theatres and films, had her long hair cut fashionably short, and bought two new outfits. All in all, the following fortnight passed quickly. Tony returned at the weekend with the news that his father was on the mend, but that he was going to leave London and return to the family business, a small engineering works outside Oxford—and Maria, as gently as she could, told him that while she would want to stay friends with him, she could see no future for them together. He took it badly, but not as badly as she had feared. He was ambitious, had only left Oxford because he and his father clashed on nearly everything, but now that the situation had changed and his father had been warned by doctors to ease the pressure, things would be different. It was with a sense of loss that Maria said goodbye to him finally, knowing that in a while he would find someone else. He was young, only twenty-five, attractive and confident. His heart was bruised, not broken.

And also, during that fortnight, she had a letter from Craighowe Garage to say that her car was repaired, the damage had not been as bad as feared, it would cost her ninety-eight pounds, and would she be good enough to let them know when she would collect?

She telephoned them from work one day and told them that, as it was difficult at the moment to get away, would they mind garaging it until she could get up. She would of course, she told them, pay for the service, and was informed by the softly spoken proprietor that it would be no trouble at all, for a few weeks at any rate.

That was that. She had practically forgotten about her precious Mini, usually keeping it garaged at the back of the flats and driving only at weekends. She didn't feel happy in London traffic anyway and found buses or underground sufficient for all her needs.

Life was getting hectic. November came, and with it mists and frosty mornings walking to the underground for her train to work, and parties and long evenings talking to Cassie and other friends. She went out several times with men that she knew and liked, but there was nothing personal in the dates. She would have a pleasant evening, and they would see her home, but she rarely invited any in for coffee, only those she trusted. And it began to work. Brand was still there at the background of her being, but she was not consciously aware of thinking about him. Only the dreams, but she couldn't do anything about those, and rarely remembered them after being awake a few minutes.

Everything seemed to be under control. Until the day Brand came into the office to see Mike. . . .

They were all busy, swapping ideas, going over a campaign for a new brand of chocolates that was to be launched nationwide the following Easter. Newspaper ads, television, hoardings, magazines. The launch was to be a complex and expensive one, and everyone actively engaged in the creative process was involved.

Maria, wrestling with a cardboard cut-out that refused to obey her nimble fingers, was swearing softly under her breath when Harry whispered in her ear: 'The girl on the switch says the big man himself's on the way in.'

She looked up. 'Who? What "big man"?'

'*The* boss, the new owner. The one to whom even Mike is reputed to genuflect.'

She went very cold. 'How does the switch girl know that?' she asked, trying hard to control the hammering of her heart. She could almost sense the whispers going round the office, the air of excitement, like a buzz of activity as everyone became extremely busy.

'The naughty girl listened in, didn't she?' he said, affecting disapproval with pursed lips. ''Cos he sounded so incredibly sexy, *she* says, that she wondered who it was. Name's Cadell——'

'Cordell,' Maria corrected, and he smirked.

'Got you! Know him, do you?'

'Don't be silly.' She tried to laugh. 'Anyway, hadn't you better get back to work?'

'Yes.' He slid off her desk. 'God, this new chocolate campaign is giving me a headache. I wouldn't mind if it was good, but did you taste the sample? Ugh!' He pulled a face and strolled away, whistling.

Maria picked up her handbag and went out to the ladies' room. Brand had said he would never be going in. What did it matter anyway? He would probably ignore her completely. At the very most, a 'good morning', or a casual nod.

He'd be with Mike in his office, perhaps not even look in. She hoped not. She didn't want to see him again. In the three weeks since she had seen him, she had changed so much. She didn't want all the good work to be undone.

Her fingers were shaking slightly as she smoothed on lipstick and combed her hair. The new short style had been greeted by everyone with enthusiasm. Brand might, with a little luck, not even recognise her.

That was a stupid thought, but at least it made her smile at her reflection before turning away. The door burst open and Jenny, the typist, flew in, eyes wide. 'Wow!' she gasped. 'Have you *seen* him! Cor, Maria, he's dishy!' She scrabbled in her bag for a lipstick and began to put it on.

'He's here?'

'Yes. Came through with Mike on their way to Mike's office. Said good morning *ever* so charmingly and smiled. He looked a bit shy.' She blew a kiss at her reflection in the mirror. Shy? *Him?*

'Shy?' Maria echoed. 'What makes you say that?'

'Well,' Jenny tugged at her panty hose and rubbed her lips together to smooth in the colour, 'he—ouch!— gosh, I must lose some weight—he looked round as if he wasn't used to going in big offices—well, not really *shy*, I don't suppose, more—well——' she pulled a face, 'well, like looking round at everything. Taking it all in, you know.'

'Hmm—well, he would be, wouldn't he, he's never been in before,' Maria agreed.

'Mike pointed at your desk.' Jenny's eyes widened. 'Hadn't you better get back in there?' She giggled. 'You don't want him telling you off for spending all day in here. Come on. You've missed him now, but he'll call in when he's going, with a bit of luck.'

'I'll follow you in a moment, Jenny. Just got to pop to the loo,' Maria said. Something had just come to her. As Jenny darted out she looked at herself in the mirror and said softly: 'The new me, remember?'

Why should she *avoid* Brand Cordell? There was absolutely no reason at all. He had been instrumental in persuading her to stay. That was what being a shrewd businessman was all about, and she did her work well, with enthusiasm, because she enjoyed it. But she owed him nothing, nor he her. And he was involved with a glamorous woman. When—*if*—she met him today, or, for that matter, at any time in the future at the office, she would speak calmly and courteously, as befitted employee to owner. Whatever had been—and it was little enough—between them was well and truly over, and the sooner she was able to react normally at the sight of him the better it would be.

She took a deep breath, a final flick at an unruly bit of hair with her fingers, and went out.

Work continued. Lunch came and went, and no one knew whether or not Brand was still closeted in Mike's office. There was another way out, and if they had gone that way, as they surely must have for lunch, there was no reason to suppose Brand would return. Maria wished she hadn't known about his arrival at all. It was all very well, she decided, to be calm and serene when he came in, but not knowing whether he would or not was having a slightly deleterious effect on her concentration.

It was nearly four. Harry had brought her a cup of coffee, and sat on her desk smoking while he drank his. The atmosphere in the office was back to normal. Everyone save Maria had assumed that Brand and Mike were out drinking and lunching late, and probably wouldn't return. As that often happened with business lunches, it was a normal and fair assumption to make.

There was the usual chatter of voices, the rapid staccato of typewriters in one corner, partitioned off from the main office, a friendly squabble over the wording

of a washing up liquid jingle going on in one corner—
all in all, a normal Wednesday afternoon.

Then the door to the corridor which led to Mike's
office opened and his head came round. 'Harry,' he
called, 'can I have a word?'

Harry slid his long legs to the floor. 'Coming.' He
raised his eyebrows at Maria. 'This is it,' he said in a
theatrical whisper as Mike disappeared. 'If I don't
come back, tell them I died bravely——' clutching his
head he staggered out.

There had been a momentary pause in the noise
when the door had opened. It resumed as Harry went
out. No one was taking any more notice. But Maria
wondered. Was it just Mike who wanted to see Harry,
or was Brand still there? Either would be logical.
Harry was the senior member of the think tank, having
worked there for seven years, and was often consulted
when something new came up. She finished her coffee
and started work again.

She had nearly forgotten about Harry when he returned, came over to her desk, and said: 'Okay, baby,
you're next.'

It took her by surprise. She glanced up, trying to
read his expression, but he was giving nothing away.
'Who's there? Just Mike?'

He winked. 'Wait and see. Off you go.'

'Harry——' she said warningly as she stood up.

'All right, all right,' he held his hands up in surren-
der. 'Sir's with him.'

'And they want me?'

'Yup, you, my sweet.'

Right, so this was it. Metaphorically squaring her
shoulders, Maria gave Harry a lovely smile that sent
him staggering back in a pretended faint, and walked
out of the office, her head held high.

She knocked and then went into Mike's office. He

was at his large desk, cigar clamped in its usual place, and Brand was standing by the window looking out over the rooftops of London. He turned slowly at Maria's entrance and looked at her. 'Hello,' she said to him, and then, to Mike: 'Harry said you wanted to see me.'

'Yes.' Mike looked across at Brand, who nodded almost imperceptibly as Mike picked up some papers from his desk. 'Mr Cordell has been going through our accounts, and would like an individual word with all the staff about their work.'

Brand walked forward. 'Sit down, Maria,' he told her. He had a slight smile on his face, no more than that. He was behaving as though they might have met briefly, once, and Maria's new-found resolve became strengthened as she sat down and gazed at him expectantly as if she too found him a faintly interesting stranger. 'I've been looking through some of the promotions you've handled and I'm most impressed.'

'Thank you—sir,' she answered quietly, the final word scarcely accentuated at all, but just enough. She saw a muscle tighten in his jaw. 'I do my best, and I enjoy my work, as I told Mr Grahame a few weeks ago.'

'I'd like to ask you something,' he said. Mike had as it were retired from the conversation. He was still in the room, but he might as well not have been. He sat very still apparently reading a memo from off his desk, only the slight movement of his cigar betraying the fact that he hadn't actually turned to stone.

'Yes, what is it?' Her tone was bright, politely curious.

'How do you feel about a rather delicate job that will entail your travelling?'

'I'm sorry?' She was bewildered. Was he going to ask her to supervise poster hoardings in busy high streets? That was the first absurd idea that came to her mind. Dismissed instantly of course, but still——

'I should explain more clearly. I have a very old and dear—friend who lives outside Edinburgh. He owns a couple of old-established and thriving businesses manufacturing kitchenware and furniture, and until now has jogged along happily with common-or-garden ads on T.V. and in papers. Recently he himself made a breakthrough by inventing a work-saving product for the busy housewife. It needs a new approach in advertising and he wants to launch it in a big way. What I am saying is in strict confidence, by the way, do I make myself clear?'

Maria nodded. 'Quite clear.'

'Good. I've suggested that you go up there and discuss it—see the "product" in action and plan accordingly. You, as a woman, will approach it from a woman's angle. Too many things in the pa t have been not only designed but advertised by men  and it takes a woman to understand another woman's point of view.'

'What is the "product"?' she interrupted.

'I thought you'd ask.' He smiled slightly. 'It's a new design of pan set—something similar to a pressure cooker, but different altogether in concept and originality. It needs someone to use it—and Mike tells me you're an excellent cook.'

She spared Mike a brief glance that should have shrivelled him, and probably would have, had he not by then been concentrating on reading yet another memo. Maria had once had Mike and his wife over for dinner. She wished now that she hadn't bothered. He was a traitor.

'Thank you, Mike,' she said in a voice that dripped icicles. He looked up and grinned idiotically at her. Turning to Brand, she added in pleasant tones: 'I'm very flattered that I've been asked, but I'm sure there are others here you would prefer, because they're far more experienced than I. And,' she added, 'you have an agency in Edinburgh. That would be far more handy for your friend.'

'No. I've been up there, and there's no one there who'll do.' He turned to Mike, who was looking ever so slightly uncomfortable, to his credit. 'Mike, do you think you could arrange to have coffee sent in to us? This could take several more minutes.'

'Sure.' Mike lumbered to his feet, clearly a relieved man. 'I'll go and see——' his voice faded as the door closed after him. There was a brief pause, then Maria said, very firmly:

'The answer's no. Did you think I'd agree? I don't know what your reasons are, and I don't want to. I was persuaded to stay on here, and I've done so, and that's fine. But this—no.'

'I see.' Brand pulled Mike's chair away from the desk and sat down. He leaned back in the padded leather swivel chair and regarded her assessingly. 'I don't suppose extra money would persuade you?'

She looked at him contemptuously. 'You'll have to do better than that. I have enough for my needs.'

'Then if I tell you something I didn't intend to, will you listen?'

'I'll listen.'

'The man—Charles Forrest—is more than just an old friend. He is—was—a cousin of my mother's. They actually worked together in a lighthearted way for several years.' He paused. 'Your father was involved too. That is, in a sense, why I'm asking you.'

Maria's face had gone white. 'How—how do you know that?' she whispered.

'It's only since a visit to Charles that I learned of the connection. I thought, as you did, that no one had ever known about my mother's and your father's long relationship, but I was wrong. Charles knew. He'd met your father, and they stayed with him occasionally, breaking their journey to Rhu-na-Bidh—he'd known for years, and he had——' he paused as if he found difficulty in composing the words, 'had never told anyone.'

Maria, shaken, raised anguished eyes to meet his. 'Why have you told me now?' she asked.

'He was talking to me, describing my mother's enthusiasm, her joy, in the new "toy" he'd invented—and the name slipped out. He said, "Hugo was very keen——". I knew then, and I asked him, but he clammed up instantly, so I told him——' He stopped talking, rose, and went over to the window. With his back to Maria he went on: 'I told him that I knew everything, that I'd had to go to the cottage to sort out papers. It was as if a dam burst. It all came pouring out—his love for them both, his concern about the cottage—everything—his sadness. He thought he was the only one who knew, you see.' He turned round to face her. 'I would like you to meet him. Do you know why, now?'

'Yes,' she answered softly. 'Yes, I do. I—I thank you for telling me.' She gazed into his eyes. 'When would you like me to go?'

Brand smiled for the first time. 'As soon as you like. Can you manage this weekend?'

She nodded. 'How long will I be there?'

'A week, perhaps more. You'll be a free agent. You'll decide. I'll take you up there.'

'No.' She shook her head. 'I prefer to go by train.'

'Train? What about your car?'

'It's ready. I might—it might be a good opportunity to collect it. I'll see,' she shrugged.

'That sounds reasonable. The island is only a hundred miles or so farther on—you can take an extra day or so after.'

'Yes. Thank you.'

'But I'll still take you to Charles' house. I'm expected—and you'd never find it.'

'You'd be surprised, Mr Cordell,' Maria told him.
'I'm quite bright at finding my way about, and I dare
say I can buy an A to Z guide for Edinburgh. I believe
they don't cost a fortune.'

His mouth twisted. 'You never give up, do you?'

'No.' She met his hard grey eyes expressionlessly. 'I
don't.'

'It's several miles north of the city, not on an A to
Z.'

'Shame. Never mind, I'll get a taxi, and put it down
on expenses.'

Brand suddenly banged his fist on the desk. 'Are
you going or not?' he demanded.

'Yes, I've said so. But only because——' she hesitated, 'because of the associations——'

'Then you will go with me.'

The door opened and Mike walked in. It seemed
almost as if he had timed it. His arrival could not have
come at a better moment as far as Brand was concerned. Three cups of coffee were on the tray he
carried, and Brand said smoothly: 'Just what we
needed. Maria's agreed. We leave on Friday. She may
be away for a week or more.'

'Good, good,' Mike agreed heartily—too heartily.

Brand looked at his watch. 'Good grief, is that the
time?' He drank his hot coffee. 'I must go.'

To Fortnum's perhaps? thought Maria. She stood
up. 'I'd better go too. I have something to finish
before I leave tonight.'

As she walked towards the door, Brand asked her:
'Can you be ready at ten on Friday?'

'Morning?'

'Yes.'

'I'll be ready. Here—or at home?'

'At home.'

Maria took a deep breath. 'I'll be there. Goodbye.' She walked out.

It was Friday morning. Maria packed a suitcase, wrote a note for the milkman, and went up to tell Cassie that she would be leaving within half an hour.

'You mean he's coming here!' Cassie's eyebrows nearly vanished. 'How *do* you do it, darling?' she drawled.

'Believe me, it's not what you think,' but Maria couldn't help laughing at Cassie's expression as she said it.

'No, of course not.' Cassie put on a suitably solemn face.

'It isn't. I'll be working, honestly.'

'*I* believe you. Did I say I didn't?' She was all wide-eyed innocence.

Maria shook her head. 'You're impossible!'

'I know, love, I know. But it's fun.' Cassie lowered her voice. 'Be good—and if you can't be good, be careful.'

'I do know the rest of that advice, and I *assure* you there's no way I——'

'Hmm. No?'

'No. This is business, strictly business. The fact that he insists on driving me there is nothing. I should imagine he'll stay overnight, then return to London. He does, after all, have a very glamorous girl-friend here.'

Cassie pulled a face. 'Mmm, so he has, the beast.'

Maria laughed. 'It helps, believe it or not. There's nothing more guaranteed to bring anyone down to earth as seeing someone looking like her attached to the man you think you're in love with.'

She regarded herself in the long mirror on Cassie's

wall. She had, admittedly, dressed in her best suit, a slim-fitting jacket and skirt in a soft rose pink, with a cream-coloured blouse, and her long, long legs were clad in extremely sheer hose, but that was simply because she felt better when she looked smart, she told herself. Her new short hairstyle framed her face softly, she was pleased to note. She drew herself up to her full height and affected a haughty pose, at which Cassie clapped her hands. 'Actually, love, you look extremely glamorous yourself today. May I suggest a touch of dramatic eye make-up to complete the stunning picture?'

'Why not! Have we time?'

'Of course we have. Find a chair. I've got all the latest stuff, including kohl liners and a goldy brown shadow that's guaranteed to knock 'em out.'

Twenty minutes later, when a bell shrilled from downstairs, a cool, calm Cassie said: 'Stay here, I'll get it. It won't hurt him to wait a minute. Put the kettle on.'

'But——' protested Maria.

'Shut up. Do as you're told. When he comes in, be standing in the doorway from the kitchen holding a tea towel.'

'But——'

'And leave the rest to me.' Cassie went out in a swirl of kaftan, leaving a rather bemused and bewildered Maria to do exactly as she was told.

# CHAPTER NINE

POSING in the doorway to the kitchen, holding a tea towel as per instructions, Maria waited, stifling a giggle. She knew Cassie well enough to know that she wouldn't let her down. Cassie could switch on an elegant lady act to delight her friends at the drop of a hat. There were no hats to drop, but that didn't matter. It felt, Maria decided, like waiting on stage for curtain up.

She heard the voices from the stairs coming nearer, Cassie speaking in her low, gentle, terribly posh tones but not overdone at all. She could fool anyone, even him. '—I insist, Mr Cordell, Maria's making coffee now. Just one more flight, that's it. Oh, Orlando, you silly boy!' a gentle, low-pitched laugh followed. 'I hope you don't object to cats. I have three.'

'Not at all.' Cassie swept in with a flourish and ushered Brand in. Maria, trying to give the impression of having just moved from the kitchen on hearing them enter, smiled at Brand.

'Good morning,' she said.

'Good morning, Maria.' He was dressed in the grey suit she had last seen him in outside Fortnum's. 'Are you nearly ready to travel?'

'Yes.' He was looking at her very coolly and assessingly.

'But we're all having coffee first. Do sit down, Mr Cordell.' Cassie swept several papers off the nearest normal chair and gave him her sweetest smile. 'If any of the cats try to jump on your knee, just push them away. I'd hate you to get cat hairs on that beautiful suit.'

He laughed. 'I think it could take it.'

'I'll help you—excuse us a moment, Mr Cordell, won't you?' In the kitchen, out of his view, she winked at Maria, silently mouthed the words: 'Very nice,' then said loudly; 'Do you take sugar?'

'No, thanks.'

Two minutes later they were all seated. Brand had accepted his bowl of coffee without the slightest display of surprise, quite as though he drank thus every day. Cassie lounged on her beanbag, and Maria sat on the only other "normal" chair in the room. Brand had been looking round him while they had been making the coffee, and now said: 'I see you're an illustrator, Miss Farr——'

'Cassie, please.'

'Cassie. Is it for some magazine?'

'Several, actually. Mainly the teenage market.'

'Interesting,' he observed.

'It is. I love the work. You could say that Maria and I are in a similar line of business, although hers is by far the most creative.' She gave Maria a pleasant little smile. 'And you own her company. I find that fascinating. Are you involved with the day-to-day running of the agency yourself, Mr Cordell?'

'Brand,' he corrected. 'Please. No, unfortunately I don't have as much time as I'd like. But the man in charge, Mike Grahame, is very capable, as I'm sure Maria would be the first to agree.'

'Yes, he is,' she agreed dryly. Capable of a little gentle blackmail too, when called for, she thought.

'You have other business interests, Brand?' Cassie was all wide-eyed interest, her huge glasses lending her an air of demure innocence.

'Several,' he agreed. 'All rather boring.' And he gave her a pleasant smile to let her see that he also found it rather boring to talk about. Cassie wasn't so easily deterred, however.

'Oh dear, not in advertising? Let me guess. Banking?'

He laughed. 'You're a shrewd lady, aren't you?'

'I'm right?'

'Yes, you're right. But not in England—abroad. Which is why I travel quite a lot.'

Maria had gathered what Cassie was up to minutes previously. What she didn't understand was why. Cassie sighed. 'And you call that boring? I find it fascinating.'

'Facts and figures and money are very dull stuff compared to advertising.'

'Perhaps to you. Are you going to spend more time in future with Prothero and Michaels?'

Brand glanced across at Maria. It was a brief but eloquent glance. He assumed she had put Cassie up to it. Maria was about to speak when Cassie did so for her. 'You must forgive me. I'm a very nosey character, as Maria knows only too well.' She laughed. 'And inviting you for coffee and then questioning you is not what being the perfect hostess is all about. It's just that I'm interested in everything about people.' She blinked, then lowered her eyes submissively. 'Am I forgiven for prying?'

'Of course. There's nothing to forgive. I'll answer your question—no, I'm not going to spend more time with the agency, and even if I could, I wouldn't.' He paused, turned his head slightly to look at Maria, who sat, poised, long legs elegantly crossed at the ankles, sipping her coffee as though this had nothing to do with her at all. 'Because I've always found it good policy never to interfere when something is as smooth-running as the agency obviously is. There may be some staff changes, however—and this is in confidence for the moment. I've been studying the market, and there's great scope for a branch in the North. I may be opening one near York in the near future. If—when—I do, there's a member of the London staff who would be keen to go. He's a Northerner himself, and most of his relatives are there.'

'Harry,' Maria said quietly.

'Yes. I've spoken to him already. In that event, there'll be a step up for another member of staff.' He looked straight at Maria, and this time it was as though Cassie wasn't there. There might have been just the two of them in the room. 'Would you be interested, Maria?'

'This is a bit sudden,' she admitted, to give herself time to think.

'I know. I didn't intend to tell you yet, but your charming friend,' he gave Cassie a wry grin, 'has a knack of making people say things—as I'm sure she's well aware.'

'Oh, Maria! What an opportunity!' Cassie gasped. Her cut-glass accent had faded slightly in her excitement.

'I don't expect an answer. It's all very much in the air at the moment, but at the beginning of next year I'll be exploring all the possibilities.'

'Then we'll leave it till then,' Maria said quietly. 'Thank you for asking. I'm well aware of the compliment—but I must tell you there are some in the office who've been there longer than me.'

'I judge by ability, not length of service, Maria,' he said. At the same time that the conversation was happening, one part of Maria's mind had as it were stepped back to observe this man. What greater contrast could be imagined between him as he was now, and as he had been at the cottage? Cool, incisive, razor-sharp mind, a man to respect. As at home here as he would be in the finest restaurant or mansion. Polite and courteous too, he had been more than a match for Cassie's questions—and Maria didn't doubt that, had he chosen, he would have told her nothing about himself, without the slightest appearance of rudeness. And in that case, why had he? He had said more than was necessary, and he must therefore have a reason. Was it because he knew what the answer would have been if he had asked Maria when they were alone? Could it be that he played Cassie's own cleverness back at her by gaining an ally? Anything was possible, with him. He was an expert verbal fencer.

He looked at his watch, not obviously, but as if concerned about the time. Then to Cassie he said: 'I'm enjoying talking to you, Cassie, and the coffee was delightful, but I think we'll have to tear ourselves away very soon. There's a restaurant near Lancaster I'd like to have lunch at, and it's quite a way away.'

'Of course.' Cassie, ever the perfect hostess, rose to her feet and took his empty bowl. 'And I've enjoyed meeting you very much. You must come again—perhaps some evening to one of my little *soirées*.'

'I'd be delighted,' he said, with charm and, Maria knew, total insincerity. He bent and picked up Cleopatra who had been waiting patiently to get into his chair, and put her on it. Then he held out his hand to Cassie. 'Thanks again, Cassie. Is your case here, Maria?'

'No, in my flat. I'll collect it on the way down.' She hugged Cassie. 'I'll see you soon, love.'

'Yes. Oh, had you better leave your phone number in case I get any messages?'

Maria looked at Brand. She didn't even know exactly where they were going. He produced a visiting card from his breast pocket, scribbled a number on, and handed it to Cassie.

'Thanks.' She studied it, then put it behind the clock on the mantel. 'Off you go, then. Have a safe journey and enjoy your lunch.'

'We will. Goodbye.'

'*Au revoir*,' Cassie returned, and watched them out. As they went down the stairs, she was singing a little tune to herself.

'I'll wait in the car,' Brand told Maria, 'unless your case is heavy?'

'No. I'll be down in a minute.' She let him go on down, opened her flat door, and went in.

Minutes later they were on their way, not in the Land Rover she had half expected would be waiting, but in a new maroon Jaguar sports car.

'You've had your hair cut,' he said, after a few miles had passed. Soft music from a stereo tape filled the car, and conversation was mercifully unnecessary.

'Yes. It's part of the new me,' she responded flippantly. She had no intention of asking him if he liked it.

'It suits you,' he said after a few moments during which he glanced sideways at her. 'Makes you look younger.'

'Thank you.'

'New outfit?'

She looked down and brushed a few cat hairs from the skirt. 'Yes.'

'It's very chic.'

'Thank you again.' She glanced out of the window. This was the Brand with whom she could be quite at ease. Whether or not he was going out of his way to make her feel so didn't matter. There was none of the tension she had secretly dreaded. If he was going to behave like this, and as he had in Cassie's flat, all the way to Edinburgh, the journey would be a pleasant one. And if ever she caught herself feeling faintly in love with him, she had only to conjure up the image of that oh-so-attractive woman he had been escorting and it would go away quickly. All in all, things might not be so awful.

'Cassie's an interesting woman, isn't she?' he commented. 'Have you known her long?'

'Several years. She's a good friend.'

'I'm sure she is.' There was silence again. The tape

was of guitar music, and soothing, faintly romantic. It filled the car, but not loudly, and Maria listened, letting it flow round her and soothe her senses with the richness of the *Concierto de Aranjuez* by Rodrigo. It was one of her favourite pieces, and she hummed it under her breath. Golden music, spilling out, almost sensual. She closed her eyes, the better to listen, and perhaps Brand realised, for he didn't speak again until it had finished, when he said:

'Is that one of your favourites too?'

'Yes, it is. It's quite beautiful.'

'Do you like classical music?'

'Quite a lot. I'm not so keen on Beethoven—why?'

'There's a box of tapes under your seat. Choose what you want.'

Maria bent down and brought out a vinyl-covered case. The next few minutes were occupied in searching through it. She was surprised at his taste—not because it was bizarre, but because it reflected her own so closely. Tchaikovsky, Mozart, Grieg, Wagner—all were there. She selected three and he said: 'Tell me what you've chosen.'

'Er—Hebridean Overture, Italian Symphony, Bruch Violin Concerto.'

'They're your favourites?'

'Yes. There are more, but these will last until we stop for lunch, I should imagine.'

He laughed. 'Very possibly. We have similar tastes in music. Put them in the glove compartment for now.'

They were nearing the motorway and he increased speed subtly and skilfully until they were doing well over ninety. 'If I'm going too fast for you, say so,' he told her.

'I don't mind. As long as you're a good driver, and I've no reason to think you're not.'

'You will, of course, watch out for police cars,' he said.

'Of course,' she answered dryly. 'Have you ever been stopped?'

'No. But I'm not stupid enough to think it can't happen.' Nothing had passed them since their motorway journey began. Cars in the other two lanes seemed almost at a crawl, yet Maria was totally relaxed. There was no sensation of speed. If she hadn't glanced at the speedometer she would have guessed they were doing no more than sixty.

There was something she wanted to know, and in the pause while she changed tapes she said: 'Are you going back to London as soon as you've left me, or stopping overnight?'

'I certainly wouldn't travel back tonight. As for the rest of the time, I've not decided.'

Not decided? What did he mean? 'Oh, you mean you might stay there the weekend?'

'Or longer.'

She digested the two words in silence. Perhaps his red-haired mistress had gone away. She could hardly ask *that*. 'But,' she said, after a few moments' pause while she had started the tape, 'you've got to get back for business, haven't you?'

'No. Everything's running smoothly in all of my— commitments.' There was a subtle pause before the last word. 'And I believe in letting those I employ get on with it in their own way.'

'I know what you mean. I work best alone,' she answered. It seemed a tactful way of letting him know that she didn't want him, without actually saying so, because the sparks weren't flying, and she had no intention of starting them off.

'Do you? I thought it might be interesting to see the way your mind worked.'

She didn't understand him at all. He had, on more than one occasion, made his feelings towards her perfectly clear, as she had to him. He was not an insensitive man—and yet he had just said this.

'You mean you're actually going to *stay*?' she asked.

'Very possibly.'

'Look,' she said, 'I work for you—still—because you persuaded Mike Grahame, of whom I am very fond, to talk me out of leaving. You did a very good job on him too, I've got to hand you that. He seemed to think you had a never-ending whisky bottle——'

She was halted by his laughter, which strangely angered her. She bit her lip, determined not to lose her temper. It wasn't easy. 'Did he say that?' Brand managed, when the laughter had died down.

'Yes,' she said tartly. 'He did. He's nobody's fool either. I hope you've given him his raise——' She hadn't intended to say that.

'It's all been taken care of. I don't go back on my word, Maria.'

'Yes, you do,' she retorted, keeping her voice calm, but only with difficulty. 'You said you wouldn't call in at the office.'

'I had to, to see Harry—and to ask you to do this special favour for me. If I had telephoned you to ask you to dinner with me, would you have come?'

'No.'

'Then I had no choice, did I, but to see you at work?'

She didn't answer him, and he repeated: 'Did I?'

'No,' she answered. 'But—you know why——' she stopped.

'I only know that some things are best forgotten. Grow up, Maria. You're a mature woman who happens to be very good at her job. You're creative, you

have the talent and skill to put adverts together, to
sell products to the Great British Public—and that's
what it's all about, remember. I happen, by reason of
inheritance, to own the place that employs you, I've
seen your work, talked to your immediate boss, Mike,
who is, as you remarked, nobody's fool, and *I* would
have been the fool to let you go. Can we take it from
there? Can we agree to put out of our minds the
unfortunate and tragic circumstances of our initial
meeting and get on with the business we both want to
do?'

He was slowing, drawing into a motorway service
station, and in the full car park he found a place,
backed into it, and stopped the car. Then he looked at
her, and she met his eyes, reluctantly, but compelled
to. There was the faintest scar on his forehead, just
under the hairline, skin paler in a thin ribbon, almost
concealed by his hair. That jolted her memory in a
strange way, and she shivered very slightly.

'We've both said things that we regretted,' Brand
went on. 'I'm a proud man, but I can admit when I
was wrong. And once admitted, I don't brood about it.
Neither should you. This weekend, and next week,
you'll be working on something that I hope you'll find
satisfying. The man you cared most about and the
woman I cared most about were involved in it too. For
that reason, and the other reasons I've just given you,
about your skill and imagination, I've chosen you to
think up a campaign that will sell the product. You'll
have help—if you need it—but if you work best alone,
and I accept for you it's the best way, then you'll have
the time and privacy you need. I will respect your
wishes on that.'

He paused. His eyes were hard and bleak, as Maria
well remembered from previous occasions. She took a
long, shuddering breath. His words had the strong

effect on her that he intended.

She nodded. 'I'm sorry. You're right, of course, in all you say. You've made me see things differently, and I'm glad you have. I'll work hard—and I won't let you down.' It was her turn to pause, to search now for the right words. 'And if—if it's important to you— if you want to, that is, I'll discuss things as we go along. I can do that. Often in the office we bandy ideas about, and it helps. Two or more minds can come up with ideas, working together, that would take one person longer. Are *you* creative?'

He smiled, he actually *smiled*. 'I like to think so. But, frankly, this is new to me—I'd be very much a bumbling amateur compared to you, but—I'd like to try. If you'll give me a chance.' There was no arrogance in his words. There was no sarcasm either, as there could well have been—there were just the words, simply stated, of a man successful beyond her imagining, who was prepared to learn.

'You're my employer,' she murmured, still feeling slightly stunned. 'I can hardly talk of "giving you a chance" as though you were some new office boy.'

'Can we forget that I'm your boss for a while? Can *you* forget?'

'Not easily,' she admitted.

'Then try. For this next week we're two people who've met for the purpose of creative work, no more than that. You're an expert, I'm a beginner—but a very quick learner. Everything else is to be forgotten. London—the cottage—the agency. Okay?'

'Okay.'

'Then let's go and have a cup of doubtless abysmal motorway coffee before we continue our journey.'

'All right.' Maria unfastened her seat belt and opened the door.

It was nearly dark when they arrived at Inchcape House, but even in the dusky gloom of a late November afternoon Maria could see how beautiful it was. A tall stone-built mansion in several acres of gardens, it stood aloof and dignified at the end of a long winding drive. Lights blazed from several windows and from the colonnaded entrance, and she made a murmur of pleasure. 'What a gorgeous place,' she said.

'It's even better inside. Let's get in out of the cold.' It was indeed freezing cold, and she waited, shivering, as Brand opened the trunk and took out their cases. The door was flung open and she turned towards it to see a man advancing towards them. Tall, grey-haired, with a moustache, he was smiling broadly.

'Hello,' he greeted them, and Brand put down the cases.

'Maria, my cousin Charles Forrest. Charles, Maria Fulford.'

He took her hand in a hearty grip. 'I'm very pleased to meet you, Maria,' he said. 'Very pleased indeed. Come along in with me and get out of the cold and let me look at you.'

He ushered her in, leaving Brand to follow, and led her into a large hall gleaming with light from a beautiful chandelier. The carpet was warm red and welcoming, and a blazing log fire threw out heat.

'How lovely!' she exclaimed.

'Come on in here. I'll show you round later.' Brand came in, put the cases by the entrance, and followed them into a large comfortably furnished drawing room. The lighting was more subdued here, wall sconces lending a more intimate atmosphere to the room with its beautiful antique furniture.

'Sit you down by the fire. What'll it be for you, Maria? Sherry, Martini—name it, anything you want.'

'Dry Martini, please,' she answered, liking the man.

Rosy-cheeked, blue-eyed, with an infectious smile, he was altogether delightful. She looked round the room as Brand went to stand near the fire. Her father had been here and met this man, been a guest in the house. She felt as if she knew him well, although they had only just met.

He handed her a large crystal goblet. 'There you are. Get that down you—Brand, I know what you'll have, so don't tell me.'

He poured out two whiskies and handed one to Brand. Then he raised his glass. 'Good health—and success on our little enterprise.'

They raised glasses and drank, murmuring their responses, and Charles beamed benevolently at them both. 'This is going to be a successful week,' he said. 'I feel it in my bones. Maria, Brand tells me you're damned good at your job—just wait and see where you're going to work. I think you'll like it.'

'I'm sure I shall,' she answered.

'She's got to try the cookers first,' said Brand, 'and I was assured by Mike Grahame that she's a good cook.'

'Are you now?' Charles swallowed his whisky. 'I can see we'll have to have a tour of the kitchen first. My housekeeper's away for the weekend and I've got a temporary woman from the village who'll be delighted to let someone else do the cooking occasionally.' He winced. 'So will I. She means well, and she does her best, but it's very basic fare. Thank God my housekeeper prepared us a slap-up meal before she left.' He sat down next to Maria. 'We'll eat at seven-thirty. Would you like to go up to your room to freshen up first?'

'I'd love to.'

'Good. Brand, show Maria up, will you? I've put her in the pink room—you've got your own little bathroom, me dear, I hope you'll like the room. While you're gone, I'll just top up our glasses, so don't be long.'

Maria followed Brand along a thickly carpeted passage with wall lights glowing softly. Everywhere was immaculate. He opened a door and stood aside for her to enter.

'Here you are.'

She looked around her. The walls were a deep pink, in gold-bordered oblong panels, the rest of the walls and the ceiling a paler, toning pink. The shades on the wall lamps were pink as well, as was the light by the side of the huge bed. 'It's absolutely beautiful,' she said.

'Isn't it just?' He pointed to a panelled door at the far end of the room. 'That's your bathroom. Can you find your way down again?'

'I'll shout if I can't,' she answered. She went over to her case, which Brand had put on a chair, and he went out, closing the door. Maria drew the curtains of the large window. They were a deep pink velvet to match the deeper wall colouring. And she wasn't a bit surprised, when she went into the bathroom, to find that was pink as well. Tiles, carpet, bathroom suite, towels— and even the soap. She began to laugh helplessly, feeling absurdly happy. There was no specific reason for the feeling, it was there, that was all. But it was wonderful to be alive.

She lay in bed wide awake, too many thoughts and impressions turning in her mind to allow sleep to come. It was well past midnight and she should have been tired, but one part of the evening had been spent in the room where she was to work, and she had wandered round it, familiarising herself with the place where she would be spending many hours for the next few days. It had been originally a study. Books lined one wall, but that was all that remained of the original furnishing, save for a desk. Charles Forrest had fitted a temporary working top by the window, with huge stacks of paper, and pencils and charcoal and crayons set neatly on it. There was an adjustable typist's chair, and on the large old desk, which he had covered with a thick sheet of hardboard, were three of the pressure cookers, different sizes, and instruction leaflets. She had gone straight to the desk, after a brief glance of approval at her work surface. Both men had stood there as if waiting for instructions, and she had said: 'Please, can I just stay here for a short while alone? I'd like to study the books and examine the cookers.'

'We'll be in the drawing room,' Charles replied. 'Can I bring you a drink in?' They had already eaten their dinner.

'No, thanks. I like a clear head when I'm thinking. But when I come back I will.' She sat at the desk, not touching anything, just looking.

'I think we're superfluous,' Charles murmured, and they went out. She had stayed there for a while, examining the pans and reading the instructions with total objectivity. The ideas would come later, but at that moment she needed to discover as much as she could about them. After a while she had rejoined the two men, and they had talked about anything and everything—except the reason she was there, because she wasn't ready to talk about it yet.

Now, in her bedroom, the first idea came, and it was startling in its simplicity, and very vivid. She knew from past experience that there would be no sleep for her now until she had written everything down. She knew her way to the workroom, because it was almost directly below her room, on the ground floor.

Maria put on her dressing gown and slippers, opened the door, and crept very quietly down the stairs. She switched on the light in the workroom, pulled the chair up to her work surface, grabbed paper and pen and began to write. Her hand couldn't keep up with her thoughts and the words tumbled out on to the paper in a scribble. 'Damn, oh damn!' she muttered, as the pen flew across the sheet. She could do with a typewriter, or a dictaphone—or even an ordinary tape recorder.

She grabbed another sheet, a large one, and began to draw, swift sure strokes, as yet only fleeting sketches of what was on her mind. It was all so simple and *obvious*. No wonder she hadn't been able to get to sleep! With that simmering in her subconscious she had had mental indigestion. 'Good grief,' she muttered as she had to take yet another sheet of paper, 'this is ridiculous——'

'Do you always talk to yourself when you're alone?' Brand's voice came from the doorway and she turned round sharply, nearly sending a case of pencils flying.

'Oh! You scared me!' she gasped. Then: 'Don't talk. Don't say another word, please——' She turned away from him and continued the drawing she had begun. She was vaguely aware of him coming in, but it was only on the edge of her consciousness. Nothing could distract her from what she was doing now. Not until she had finished.

'Phew!' She flung down the pencil and put her head on the working top.

'May I see?' he asked.

'No!' She covered the papers. 'No—sorry. Not yet.' She looked round at him. He wore the dressing gown he had worn at the cottage, and she swallowed hard. 'It's too—amorphous yet, but I had to come down. I'd never have slept.'

'I stood at the door for ages. I've never seen anything like it before. You were scribbling away frantically, muttering to yourself.'

'Was I? Now you've seen me in action. Scared?'

'No. Impressed.' Brand shook his head. 'Incredible. Is that how it takes you?'

'Sometimes, yes. When it's right, something clicks. It's the only way I can explain it.' She put her hand to her forehead. 'Oh, my poor head!'

'Headache?' he queried.

'Not exactly. And my hand—talk about writer's cramp!' She massaged her right hand gently.

He laughed. 'And you enjoy your work? Sounds painful to me.'

She smiled. 'It is sometimes. You've a lot to learn.' She rubbed her eyes. 'That's enough for tonight. I just had to get it down——' She sighed wearily.

'Do you want a drink of something?' he asked.

'Not alcohol—I'd love hot milk, or Horlicks, or chocolate if there is any.'

'Let's go and see. No, better still—go upstairs, I'll bring you something up—and a couple of aspirins. I think you deserve them.'

Maria nodded, too tired to argue about it. 'That'll do fine. Promise you won't look at what I've done?'

'I promise,' he said. 'Go on up.'

# CHAPTER TEN

MARIA stumbled into bed, forgetting to take off her dressing gown. Her efforts had taken their toll. She was drained and exhausted, physically and mentally. Yet there was also within her a spark of wonder at what had happened. It was a sense of complete satisfaction and rightness. The ideas might change, turn course slightly, but she had the essence of something very strong, and she had captured it on paper, in word and picture, and knew it would form the basis of the entire advertising campaign.

Before she could even begin to develop it she was going to have to try the cookers for herself, and that would be in the morning, regardless of whether the temporary housekeeper wanted to use the kitchen or not.

When Brand came in a few minutes later she had her eyes closed. She had forgotten about the drink too.

'She'll have to go,' she mumbled, and opened her eyes.

'Sorry? Who will?' He handed her a steaming beaker.

'The lady from the village, tomorrow—I mean today, I think. I'm going to be working in the kitchen—she'll have to——' her voice faded with tiredness.

'She'll have to go,' he agreed soothingly. 'I understand. Don't worry, Charles will see to it. He'll give her the day off, I shouldn't wonder.'

'Mmm——'

'Drink your milk. I put a teaspoon of honey in it,

and here are your aspirins.' He was sitting on the bed, although she hadn't remembered him doing so.

'Thanks.' She tried to look at her watch, but it was blurred. 'What's the time?'

'A little after two.'

'Good gracious, is it? I was down there over an hour?'

'Apparently. I watched from the door for over half an hour, and you never stopped once. It's no wonder your head aches.' He put his hand over her forehead. 'How is it now?'

'Terrible.' He took the beaker from her, pushed her gently back on the pillow and said:

'I'll rub the back of your neck. It'll help.'

'No, I don't think——' Maria began but oh, how nice *that* would be. And it would be quite impersonal, she knew, on Brand's part at least. She sighed, and he slid his hands round the back of her neck, ignoring that slight protest as if he hadn't heard it, which he might not have. She wasn't sure if she had actually said it, or only intended to.

'Mmm, that's better,' she murmured. 'Oh—ah——' Her eyes closed.

She already knew how gentle his hands could be. She was being soothed and pampered quite deliciously and she felt herself relaxing and almost imperceptibly losing her hold on reality.

Half dreaming as she was, it seemed that they were in the cottage again, sharing the bed, as they had done briefly, and she murmured: 'Put the covers over you,' because she also seemed to remember that the bedroom had been cold, although it wasn't now. She was very warm and comfortable. But was he? He had concussion, didn't he?

'Lie down,' she said, speech blurred, and then it was just the same as it had been, and rightly so. He had to be looked after because he had got the concussion saving her luggage . . .

She turned towards him and put her hand to his face. 'Is your head better?' she asked, and he murmured:

'Yes, my love, it is, much better now,' and she snuggled up to him with a weary sigh and felt his arms go around her, then she slept . . .

Hours later she woke up to find herself in Brand's arms, and he was soundly asleep. Horrified, Maria looked at the sleeping man in whose arms she lay, and she couldn't remember how he had got there.

'Brand,' she whispered fiercely, 'wake up! What are you doing here?'

He opened his eyes, as yet unfocused, and smiled at her blearily. She shook him hard. 'How did you get here?' she demanded. He was suddenly wide awake. Easing himself up, he looked down at her in bewilderment.

'God knows,' he said with feeling.

Then—*then* she remembered. 'Oh,' she whispered. 'You were rubbing my neck—I'd been working and I had a splitting headache. This is ridiculous——'

She stopped, because he was looking at her. For a few moments they neither moved nor spoke, as if incapable of either. Their warm bodies were touching, and her body was on fire, and her senses swam as their eyes met and clashed in silent challenge.

'My God,' she murmured. 'You didn't——' she began to tremble helplessly and Brand said in a husky voice:

'You wouldn't need to ask if I *had*—you'd *know*.'

She lay back and looked up at him, and he looked as though he were in pain. She made a wordless cry and gasped: 'Don't look at me like that, please——' and closed her eyes and felt his hand move across her body, then touching her neck.

'Why are you trembling?' he asked. 'It's all right. Nothing happened.'

She covered his hand with hers. 'Why are *you* trembling?' she murmured.

'Don't you know?' he whispered, and then, moments later, his mouth was on hers. 'Dear Lord, don't you *know*?' he muttered brokenly after minutes during which they clung to each other, with all their strength. Brokenly she said his name, and he buried his face in her neck, and she could feel his heart beating fast against hers. She reached up to hold his head against her, and the intensity of the fire which swept through them both consumed them utterly.

No more words were needed, for none could be said. The white-hot surging tide of excitement carried them both along with it, and this time it could be contained no longer. Their bodies became as one body, Maria cried out, once, and then no more. She was lost, utterly and absolutely, in the intensity of his love making, knowing nothing save what was happening, not even aware of her surroundings, blind with desire and the fulfilment of it, caught up in a rhythm she had never known, movement, and mounting excitement that could never end—never end ——

She lay exhausted in his arms, her heart pounding like an imprisoned bird's, and she knew that all the dreams had been as nothing compared to the reality. She closed her eyes and her heartbeats gradually slowed to normal, and sleep took her.

When next she awoke, it was morning, and she was alone. Surfacing from the depths of warm sleep, she remembered, and sat up and looked around her as if Brand might still be in the room, and her heart thudded. 'Oh, my God,' she said, out loud. She put her hand to her mouth, feeling sick, hating herself for what she had allowed to happen. Naked, she padded to the bathroom and turned on the shower, stepping under it as if to try and cleanse the memories away. She lifted her face to let the warm water splash all over her, and she ached all over, physically and mentally. How could she face him? Would he look at her knowingly, smiling, remembering how she had behaved? Or would he despise himself for losing control when he had told her once that he never did? Worst of all, what if he behaved as though absolutely nothing had happened?

She dried herself, went into the bedroom and put on her dressing gown. Brand had undressed her, skillfully and silently, and she had let him, had *helped* him ——

If she could have, she would have left, but she couldn't, because, just before he had made love to her, she had been working on something so exciting that she knew now it was right. She couldn't let Charles down. There was a bond between them, after only a few hours' acquaintance, that was instinctive, and she knew that Charles was as aware of it as she was. Whatever else happened, he was going to have an advertising campaign that would be the best thing that she had ever done.

More composed with each minute that passed, Maria began to plan her day. Brand had said that he never brooded about things that had happened, and she was going to do the same—and in a way, living in the ultra-permissive eighties, as she and he were, lovemaking was considered very lightly by most people. The fact that she had not been a part of it, until now, was immaterial. She sat and looked at herself in the dressing table mirror. Her appearance hadn't changed, she was, essentially the same person she had been yesterday. And she was no less responsible than he for

what had taken place in her bed. She had, subconsci-
ously, perhaps even consciously if she thought deeply
about it, wanted him to make love to her. And now he
had, and it was all she had imagined, and more. He
wasn't aware that she loved him, and it undoubtedly
wouldn't have made a scrap of difference if he were.
To him a physical need had been assuaged—and,
judging by his expertise, not for the first time and perhaps not even for the thousandth time.

Therefore, she reasoned, calm and logical now and
thinking very clearly because it was a question of self-
survival, what did it matter? Not one bit. To Brand,
nothing—to her, everything—now, at this moment;
but when, in a few minutes she went down to breakfast, it would be nothing to her either.

She smoothed in make-up, made up her eyes with
the things Cassie had lent her, combed her hair. She
dressed at a leisurely pace in cool casual slacks in silky
black material and an equally silky blouse in red.
Wearing red always made her feel more energetic. She
sprayed on her favourite perfume, Miss Dior, put on
her bright red, blouse-matching lipstick and was ready
to face the world, and Brand Cordell in particular.

Charles and he were in the dining room when she
went in and said a bright good morning to them both.
They both answered, and Brand got up, saying: 'Will
bacon, egg and mushrooms do you, Maria?'

'Mmm, sounds lovely. I'm starving!' She sat oppo-
site Charles, who laid down *The Times* and smiled at
her warmly.

'I've been hearing about your nocturnal activities,'
he said. 'And I must say I'm very impressed.'

For one absolutely horrific moment she thought
Brand had—then she remembered. 'Oh yes. I surprised myself,' she agreed, as a muffled clatter came
from behind her, and Brand bent to pick up two

spoons that had dropped. 'I had such a splendid idea, I knew I wouldn't sleep until I got it down on paper. So I crept downstairs to the study and started scribbling furiously.' She held up her right hand. 'This was aching so much, you can't imagine. Er—you don't happen to have a typewriter in the house, do you?'

'My dear girl, of course! How stupid of me. I'll have it moved in today. Brand was telling me you'd like the use of the kitchen today as well. Consider it yours. I'll let Mrs Hall have the weekend off and if we need any food we can send Brand for it from my restaurant in Edinburgh. So.' He sat back and beamed at her complacently. 'That's arranged. Is there anything else at all that you need?'

'Er—there may be, but you're going to think I'm mad—and you might want to know why, and just for the moment I'd rather not tell you.'

Brand placed a laden plate in front of her and she murmured her thanks. He went to sit down again and Charles said: 'For heaven's sake, ask. I'm fearfully intrigued, but I'll restrain my curiosity.'

'Well—it's a camping stove.'

'A——' he closed his mouth. 'Yes, of course. I don't have one here, but I can assure you you'll have one within the hour. I'm not an expert on the things. Are there different kinds?'

'I'm not sure myself. I'll know what I want when I see it.'

Charles looked at Brand, who appeared casually interested, no more. He was pouring himself coffee at that moment, and looked at Maria.

'Coffee?' he asked.

'Please.'

'Do you want me to take you into Edinburgh? You can choose for yourself.'

'Yes, please.' She accepted her coffee graciously.

'Thank you.' She was absolutely positive that she was behaving perfectly normally, and because of her conviction, her confidence increased subtly every moment.

'Would you, Brand? It's damned good of you. Er—I take it I'm forbidden to peep at what you've done so far?'

'Absolutely forbidden.' She grinned impishly at him. 'But I give you my word that I'll tell you both something tonight, whether all goes well or not.'

'That's fair enough,' Charles agreed. 'Mind if I smoke at table? I'm as excited as a child waiting for Christmas.'

'Of course you may,' said Maria, and he lit a cigarette. 'Don't get too optimistic. It could turn out to be no good at all——'

'Rubbish! People don't get up in the middle of the night to write as you did unless it's something special. I have absolute faith in your imaginative skill. More than that, what impresses me is the fact that you'd been here less than a night before you started getting ideas! My dear girl, you have a week ahead of you. And I will not permit you to work all the time, so let's get that straight, regardless of whether that gentleman is your employer!'

Brand acknowledged the remark with a faint smile, but said nothing. He had, Maria reflected, hardly said anything, except to offer her food and coffee. He looked tired, which was hardly surprising. He also looked pale, as if not very well. She found herself not remotely concerned about it, and wondered if she was getting tougher, or even falling out of love with him. She finished her coffee and picked up the coffee pot, and poured herself some more. That was an interesting thought to have. She would ponder on it later.

'Now,' announced Charles, 'I'll go and tell Mrs Hall·

that she's free to go home once she's tidied round, and when you return, the kitchen will be your domain for as long as you want it.' He rose to his feet. 'If you'll excuse me.'

Then they were alone. Now was the moment for Maria to establish the atmosphere that there was going to be, that there *must* be, if she were to be able to behave normally for the next few days. Brand was watching her again, face hard and still slightly pale.

'Do you *know* any shops that sell camping equipment in Edinburgh?' she asked him as if totally absorbed in her project.

'No. But Charles will have the Yellow Pages here somewhere.'

'Oh, good. There must be kinds that use Calor gas as well as the ones that use meths. I wonder, would Charles let me get more than one?'

'You have only to ask,' he said dryly. 'Your wish is his command—as I'm sure you've already noticed.'

There might have been the slightest trace of sarcasm in his tone, or there might not. 'That's fine,' she said, and reached out for a piece of toast. 'Will you pass the marmalade? Thanks.' She buttered the toast and spread marmalade liberally on it. 'My word, the air makes me hungry here,' she remarked brightly.

Brand stood up. 'If you'll excuse me, I'll go and get the directory.'

'Fine.' Maria crunched into the toast and flicked a crumb from her chin.

As he went out she let out her breath in a long silent sigh. That had not been easy. She put the toast down, suddenly not hungry. Her hand shook with a fine tremor. The worst is over, she thought. The first few minutes are always the most difficult, and they've passed now. It will get easier. It's got to. She decided she was going to persuade Charles to go with them.

She wasn't quite ready for an hour or so alone with Brand. Not yet anyway.

'Now let me see.' Maria stood in the centre of the kitchen and looked round her thoughtfully. The trip to get the camping stoves had turned into a marathon shopping spree in the end, and the fruits of their expedition lay on the table. Meat and fish, vegetables of various kinds, chicken, sausages, flour, sugar, syrup and jam and tinned meats and packets of rice, spaghetti, dried peas, lentils and soya beans. Three cookery books also sat on the table.

'This,' she told a bemused Charles, 'is what is known as a test kitchen. I shan't of course be using the camping stoves in here, but then I'll use those tomorrow—if it's not raining.'

'I'm so intrigued I can scarcely contain my curiosity,' he said. 'But I am a man of iron will power—I think! And you're certainly not going to stand outside, rain or fine, cooking on camp stoves. There's an excellent pantry with a stone floor and proper ventilation along the corridor. You can do all want in there.'

'Fine,' Maria nodded. 'Now if you'd like to leave me, I think,' she opened a few drawers, 'I think I'll find everything. If not, I'll give you a shout.'

Charles stood to attention and gave a sharp salute. 'Permission to leave, ma'am.'

'At ease, Colonel,' she lifted her chin proudly. 'Permission granted. Coffee at fifteen hundred hours, sah!' She gave an equally smart salute, and both simultaneously burst out laughing. Brand chose that moment to walk in. Maria saw his look of faint bewilderment before it vanished, and she hid a smile. Was he puzzled? That was good.

Charles wiped his eyes. 'Oh, Maria, you do me good, you really do.' He put his arm round Brand's shoulder. 'We're superfluous, old chap. Let's go and have a beer in the drawing room.' He turned as they went out. 'Shout if you need anything—ma'am.' Still chuckling, he followed Brand out.

Now she was alone. And *now* she could begin. She picked up the instruction leaflet for the cooker, perched on a stool at the table, and began to read.

Several hours later, when her arms ached, her head ached, and her feet felt as if they were on fire, she knew that she was nearer than she had ever been to the perfect, the ultimate advertisement. It would be a smasher! She picked up the leaflet, flung it up in the air, and let out a joyous whoop.

It only remained to test the two camping stoves, but her efforts at the super modern cooker had already convinced her that the results would be a foregone conclusion. The tests were a formality. She sat down, kicked her shoes off, and flopped back on the stool, against a cupboard.

She could practically see the advert on the T.V. That was cinch. The magazine advert would have to be in two parts—in colour—one on one page, the second over the page. As for the hoardings on high streets—she frowned thoughtfully. She'd work that out later—if the T.V. ads were given saturation coverage, the hoardings would only need a split picture. She nodded. 'That's it,' she said. 'That's it!'

Charles appeared in the doorway looking vaguely worried. 'Er—did you shout?' He began. 'Only I——'

Maria went over to him and hugged him. 'I've got it!' she told him. 'Oh, wait till I tell you! Mmm!' She kissed his cheek soundly. 'You're a genius!'

'I am?' He looked dazed but delighted. 'Me?'

'Yes, for inventing something so super to use! By the way, are you hungry? I've got sausage and beans and roast spuds keeping warm in your oven—*and* jam sponge pudding——'

'Sounds lovely,' he said faintly. 'You've done all those in the cooker?'

'Yes. But I'll tell you the details later.' She skipped away from him and began cleaning the table. After a moment he came forward to help her. 'Go and fetch Brand, will you? We're going to eat a belated celebration lunch. It will launch the new multi-purpose Forrest low pressure cooker—for which, incidentally, I've not yet found a name, but I've got all the adverts you'll ever need practically filmed and ready.'

'You're a marvel,' he told her.

'And so are you. Lunch will be served in five minutes.'

'With champagne.'

'With champagne,' she echoed. 'Super idea.'

She laid the table, set out the warmed plates, and waited for Brand and Charles to return. She glowed inwardly with a sense of achievement.


'That was an excellent meal,' Charles declared, refilling Maria's champagne glass. 'I've never been *much* of a man for sausage and beans myself, but knowing that they were cooked in one of my cookers gave an extra something to them. Quite delicious. What say you, Brand?'

'I quite agree,' Brand agreed, looking at Maria as he raised his glass in a mock salute. 'Delicious. Are you going to tell us about your advertising campaign?'

'Yes. But later. There's quite a lot of washing up to be done first.' She sighed. 'Back to earth.'

'Not you—me, dear. Brand and I will do that. You're to go and sit down and put your feet up. Then, when we come in, you can tell us, okay?'

'If you insist, I won't argue,' Maria grinned mischievously at them both. 'I hoped you'd offer.' She picked up her glass, precariously full, sipped some champagne, and walked out, humming the March of the Toreadors for no particular reason except that it was lively and matched her mood.

In the drawing room she lay down on the settee, closed her eyes, and fell fast asleep.

# CHAPTER ELEVEN

IT was decided to do the launch with some ceremony. Amused, Maria allowed herself to be carried along by Charles' enthusiasm, and as it approached seven, the time decided by Charles for Maria to tell them all about her plans, she found herself caught up in it.

There came a tap on her bedroom door as she washed preparatory to going downstairs to the lounge.

'Who is it?' she called, a sudden brief panic being instantly quelled.

'Me—Charles. May I come in?'

'Yes, please do. I'm quite respectable.' She looked at him. 'I was just wondering what to wear. Somehow I don't feel that trousers and blouse are quite the thing. I'll put on my suit.'

'That's why I've come. Will you allow me to make a suggestion?'

'Of course.' She was intrigued.

'My daughter, who lives down south, has several evening dresses she leaves here for when she visits. She's about your height and build, and I'm sure she'd be delighted to lend you one.'

'How very kind.' Charles had mentioned his married daughter briefly in one of their conversations. All Maria knew was that her name was Fiona.

'Come along, then. I'll show you the wardrobe and you can choose a dress.'

He led her along the corridor and opened the door to the room at the far end. He went over to the huge wardrobe and opened that.

'It's all yours,' he said.

There were at least a dozen dresses on hangers. 'I'm spoilt for choice already,' Maria confessed. 'Still, give me two minutes, okay, and I'll be down.'

'Right you are.' Charles picked up a framed photograph from a table by the window and handed it to her. 'Her wedding photo. Although I may be a doting father, I think she's very good-looking.'

Maria was looking at a tall, glamorous redhead, the picture of chic and elegance in her long white dress. A very handsome man stood by her side. Fiona was the woman Maria had seen emerging from Fortnum's with Brand.

Dazed, knowing she was expected to say something, she said:

'She's very attractive, Charles, truly.' Oh, my God, she thought.

'She and Alan—her husband—were staying with Brand a couple of weeks ago. As a matter of fact it was they who told him about my little "invention" and he came up here as a result.'

Light began to dawn, a mere glimmer at first and then a glorious burst as Maria asked him: 'Does her husband drive a Daimler?'

'Yes! How did you know?' He looked astonished.

She laughed. 'I saw her coming out of Fortnum's with Brand. She was so striking-looking I remembered her.'

'Ah yes, that's Fiona.' He sighed. 'Can't keep away from the London stores when they go. Alan's got more sense, he bribes Brand to take her on the pretext that he can never find parking spaces. And Brand, being Brand, usually obliges.' He laughed. Maria hugged him, and gave him a smacking kiss on the cheek.

'Oh, Charles, you are super!' she exclaimed.

'I don't know why, but I'm not complaining. Well, I'll let you get on. Come down when you're ready.'

She looked again at the photograph when he had gone. Dear, *dear* Fiona, she thought, I've grievously wronged you. I do most earnestly beg your pardon. She set the photograph back in its place with tender care, patted it, and went to look for a suitable dress. She liked Charles even more. He had a super daughter who was not Brand's mistress, not even his girl-friend, but a happily married woman whose husband met her from shopping expeditions in their Daimler.

She pirouetted round, dark red kaftan held to her. This was the one, no doubt about it. She closed the wardrobe and went to her bedroom to put it on.

It fitted her perfectly. Feeling extremely elegant, Maria glided down the stairs and into the drawing room. Both men stood up and looked at her, and Brand's eyes stayed upon her.

She took a deep breath, and Brand handed her a glass of champagne, bowing slightly as he did so. 'Are you ready?' he asked softly.

'I'm ready,' she answered. 'Gentlemen, your good health.' She raised her glass. This was it.

She sat down on an easy chair facing them.

'This is not going to be easy to tell,' she began, 'because I have to make you see something that's very clear in my mind—and that I'm convinced will work, by the way—simply with words, not pictures. And pictures, as we know, can tell more than any words can.' She took a deep breath. She had all their attention.

'Right. Before I begin, I'll tell you all about your low pressure cooker, and how it works—and yes, Charles, I know you thought of it, but I'm putting into my own words how I see it. First—it's very versatile, as you know. It means that an entire meal can be cooked at one time in the separate compartments, using the one lot of heat—which is very important in these economy-conscious days—and because I never believe *all* I read in any instruction leaflet, I tested it for myself. The principle is simple—and that, in a way, triggered off the whole advertising campaign. So here goes. I want you to close your eyes and imagine that you're watching television. The commercial break comes. We see a garden—this garden will do for your mental picture. It's night-time, moon on high, dark sky, trees silhouetted starkly. Standing in the middle of the lawn, outside a tent, is a woman, a duchess, let's say, wearing tiara, diamond collar, long elegant evening dress. She is standing in front of a camping stove with one of our pans on, watching it bubble and boil, and she's looking rapturous, and the voice-over says, in solemn, respectful tones; 'The Forrest Economy Cooker isn't too proud to let it be known that the Duchess uses it.' Picture changes. We see seven or eight people—all elegantly dressed, being served with a sumptuous banquet—roast lamb, vegetables, the lot, in the tent. They're all looking slightly bewildered, but clearly enjoying the meal. Picture changes again, to a luxury kitchen. Imagine this one if you like. A dozen tiny Boy Scouts, or Wolf Cubs, if you prefer, are clustered round a luxury stove watching—you've guessed it, one of your cookers bubbling away. Licking their lips in anticipation in between singing Boy Scout songs. The picture changes. A dozen Boy Scouts sitting crosslegged on the luxury kitchen floor tucking into sausages and beans with gusto, while the same voice-over says: 'Forrest Economy Cooker—the *versatile* one. The all-round cooker.'

She stopped and closed her eyes. There was a brief, pregnant silence, then Charles jumped out of his chair, came over to her and lifted her to her feet.

'By God!' he roared. 'You're a bloody marvel, Maria!' He lifted her into the air and whirled her round, shaking with laughter, nearly crying, all at the same time.

Brand rose to his feet as well. As Charles released her, dazed, he touched her arm. 'You are, you know,' he said quietly. 'That is quite a remarkable achievement.'

'Oh!' She put her hands to her face. 'Oh!' It was all she could manage. She had hoped for acceptance, but she hadn't been prepared for this.

Charles clapped Brand on the back. 'The girl's a genius, man, quite simply a genius. No wonder you wanted her to stay!'

'Oh dear.' Maria sat down, and Charles handed her a glass of champagne.

'Drink that,' he ordered. 'There's lots more, I promise you.'

She swallowed it in one and coughed as the bubbles went up her nose. 'Phew!' she spluttered. Eyes watering, she said: 'There's a bit more to do. And now you know the reason for the camping stoves. Tomorrow I'm going to cook chicken with all the trimmings, just so's *I* know it can be done. But I've no doubts about it. You've got a super idea there, Charles. I shall definitely buy one, I promise.'

'You'll have a dozen with my compliments,' he retorted.

'One will do, honestly. Well, perhaps two,' thinking of Cassie. 'Oh, and to finish off, I'll tell you how I see the magazine and poster ads tomorrow. They'll link in with the T.V. ads, of course. *And* as a final clip in the T.V. ad,' she was away again. 'A simple picture of the pan, gleaming new, with a diamond necklet draped over it, and a Boy Scout hat by the side. See?'

'I like it,' Charles nodded. 'I like it better the more I think about it. I can see it now. What did you call it?'

'I haven't thought of a name yet,' she answered. 'I said, "the Forrest Economy Cooker"—why?'

'Then you said at the end, "the versatile one. The all-round cooker".'

'Er—yes, I believe I did. I was ad-libbing, you see. The pictures were more important.' She frowned. 'Have you got an idea?'

'Something's coming. Not as good as what you've just done, but something.' Charles answered, and Brand, who had been lighting a cigar, said:

'How about "Varco"? Short for—wait for it—versatile, all round cooker?'

Charles stared hard at him. 'I like it. I *like* it!'

'So do I. It's neat, it has a certain ring to it,' added Maria truthfully.

Charles raised his glass. 'To the Varco cooker. Long may she rule in the kitchen.'

They all laughed, and Brand added: 'And on the camp site.'

Which produced further laughter, and resulted in more champagne being poured, and more, and more still. Charles, it appeared, had a vast cellar of vintage champagne and appeared to be trying to establish some sort of record for its consumption.

Maria was horrified to find, when she decided to call it a day, that she could scarcely walk. The room pitched and rolled and she clutched the chair back as both men rose to their feet to help her.

'Oh, dear,' she said. 'I feel a little——'

She seemed to be vaguely aware of Charles' voice from a great distance, saying: 'Perhaps you'd better help her, Brand. I'll tidy up here and follow you up,' but the words kept fading away and it was difficult to hear them all. She hiccupped.

'Oh, s'cuse me.'

'Come on, Maria, I'll help you,' said Brand.

Distant warning bells rang. Terribly faintly really, but loud enough for her to reply, 'I can manage——'

But she couldn't, and she heard him say something brief, and the next minute she was picked up in his arms and was being carried out of the drawing room. She closed her eyes because the ceiling had an alarming sway to it and she thought it might fall down on her, and when she opened them again she was in her bedroom lying on her bed with Brand looking down at her.

'I think—I'm a bit—tiddly,' she muttered, squinting up at him.

'I think you are,' he agreed, and sat down. 'And it's not your fault, it's Charles'—only he was celebrating your work, so I suppose it is your fault in a way.'

She giggled helplessly at that. 'Oh, you are funny,' she gasped. 'Ooh, I feel sick!'

He moved swiftly when he had to. The next moment she was in her bathroom leaning over the bowl.

'Go 'way,' she managed.

'I'll be outside.' He closed the door and left her.

A few minutes later a wiser and slightly more sober Maria came out.

'Better?' he asked.

She nodded. 'I—think so.' She closed her eyes and leaned against the doorpost.

'You'd better get to bed,' he told her.

She frowned. 'Got to—clean teeth first.'

'Go and do it then,' he said impatiently. As she went back in, closing the door, she seemed to hear a muffled oath, but she wasn't sure. She wasn't sure of anything, only that the carpet was most definitely a giant cushion that bounced beneath her feet.

He led her to the bed. 'Sit down,' he said, and knelt to take her shoes off. Maria looked at him. Something had been troubling her all evening and it seemed a good time to say it.

'I was wrong about Fiona,' she said at last. 'I didn't know she was Charles's daughter.'

Brand sat beside her. He looked puzzled. 'I'm not sure what you mean,' he said slowly and clearly as if talking to a child.

'Her. The woman I saw you coming out of Fortnum's. I thought she was your—hic—girl-friend.'

'Ah!' Light appeared to have dawned. 'Did you? Did it bother you or something?'

'I was very——' she stopped. 'No, nothing.'

'You were very no-nothing? I see.'

'No, you don't, stupid.' She put a hand to her throbbing head. 'Oh dear,' she moaned.

'Lie down,' he said gently. 'I'll help you take off your dress, then I'll go and get you some Alka-Seltzer. All right?'

'Mmm.' She wondered if he would stay with her again as he had last night. She knew she still loved him; funny how clear *that* was in her mind, because everything else was very confused. 'Yes, please.'

He eased the dress off, completely impersonally, she sensed that too, and then went out. Maria slid under the sheets and closed her eyes. Never mind, he'd be back. She had the feeling he'd gone for something, but couldn't remember what. She drifted . . .

'Drink this.' She tried to push the glass away, but Brand was persistent. To save bother, she drank the fizzy mixture obediently.

'I don't feel well,' she said, which was true. 'Don't leave me.'

'All right. Go to sleep.'

'Lie down beside me. Hold me,' she whispered.

She heard his sharply indrawn breath. 'I don't think it wise, do you?'

'Why not?'

She reached up her arms and, putting them round his neck, pulled him down, and kissed him.

'I love you,' she whispered.

'Oh, God, Maria,' he groaned. 'You don't know what you're saying.' He stroked her face. 'Dear girl, you've had too much champagne.'

'I know,' she murmured. 'I know. Don't leave me——'

He kissed her gently. 'You're going to sleep now, and in the morning you'll have forgotten all this.'

'I won't have forgotten what happened last night,' she said, and looked at him, and he saw what was in her eyes, and suddenly she wasn't drunk any more. She saw him clearly, saw the concern on his face and in his eyes, and she began to cry. Softly at first, then sobbing.

Brand held her tightly to him, rocking her gently, shushing her, and she was soothed and comforted, and the tears died away until they were completely gone.

Brand looked at her. 'Better now?'

'Mmm. I'm tired. Very tired.'

'Then you must sleep. I'll stay until you do.' He took his shoes off and sat comfortably on the bed beside her, back against headboard. Calm was in the air. Her tears had washed away all tension, and she felt very relaxed. Her eyelids grew heavy, and heavier, and in her half sleeping, half waking state it seemed that they were back at the cottage, that beautiful, magic place—as she now knew, too late. She murmured softly, and Brand took her hand. 'It's all right,' he said. 'Sleep.'

'It should have been—different,' she whispered, because thoughts were confused, past and present jumbled, colour and sound, the roaring fire at the cottage and them sitting by it drinking coffee, 'So much happened, and we never knew—it's such a beautiful place——'

'The cottage?' he asked, and it seemed natural that he knew where she meant.

'So much love there, didn't you feel it—the memories——'

'Yes, I felt it. Sleep now, my dear.'

Consciousness slipped away from her. Moments before it did she was aware that he touched, then held her hand, and it was so right, so natural, and she slid into a dreaming state, where they were in the cottage, staying there for ever and a day . . .

Bright morning light woke her from deep wonderful dreams, and she was refreshed and ready for anything. She sat up in bed and stretched her arms and yawned. She felt quite splendid. Today was big day two, the camping test day. Maria jumped out of bed and went for a shower. She was too keen to do more than drink coffee at breakfast time. Both Charles and Brand looked a little the worse for wear, not surprisingly, and she surveyed them severely across the table.

'Hangovers?' she teased. 'I'm not surprised.'

'I'm a stupid old man who should have more sense,' Charles agreed amiably, 'but you're young.' He shook his head, then winced. 'My word, but I wouldn't have changed anything that happened last night. I was even dreaming about duchesses! Bet you can't beat that, Brand?'

'I can't remember what I dreamed,' Brand answered, and his eyes met Maria's briefly. 'But I slept well.'

Maria stood up. 'I'm going into my pantry. As you now know all there is to know, you're not banned any more. In fact I may need help to get stoves going!'

'I'll be in in ten minutes,' said Charles. 'Just got to

read the headlines first.'

'All right, no hurry. I've got to decide what I'm going to prepare first. I'll be in the kitchen.'

It was going to be roast chicken, roast potatoes, peas and carrots and rich gravy made from stock, Maria decided after a delightful few minutes choosing. Might it be possible to make bread sauce as well at the same time? She debated that for a few moments before thinking—why not? In for a penny, in for a pound. Syrup pudding to follow? Again, why not?

She selected the largest sized pan and tried it for size with the chicken, with potatoes round. The separate compartment, split with dividers for the veg, the upper pan for bread sauce and syrup sponge. Charles had constructed the wonder cooker with care and precision, each compartment totally self-contained, yet removable for larger items. It was quite a work of art, and at the right price would be a boon for people in small flats with little cooking space, campers, and the economy-conscious. The secret lay in the special lid which fitted with a tight clamp. It was on the principle of the wartime 'straw box' cookers where very low heat was used to maximum effect. Maria had read about them in a book once, and been very impressed.

She began to prepare the chicken, making a herb stuffing for it, then the potatoes, and when Charles arrived all was ready for him.

She was going to use the Calor gas cooker to prepare their lunch, and for the evening meal, the other one.

The morning passed quickly, Maria checking each stage of the cooking process and making copious notes and additions to her already thick file on the Varco cooker.

Lunch was pronounced a success. Slight problems with the bread sauce were noted for future alteration, and she was having great fun wondering if a special recipe book might be produced, and, it was discussed over the table as they ate, and generally decided to be an excellent idea.

Then later in the afternoon, while they were all talking, the telephone rang, and when Charles returned it was with a worried expression. They had all been in the study, tidying up loose ends of details for the advertising campaign. He looked directly at Brand as he spoke. 'I have to leave,' he said. 'Trouble up north. I've had the accountants in at one of my factories and they've found some discrepancies in the books. I've a suspicion someone's been doing a fiddle—nothing disastrous, I assure you, but they'd like me there tomorrow.' He looked at his watch. 'Would you mind if I leave both of you? If I set out now, I'll get to Inverness by evening and can have a talk with Bill, the accountant, who's an old friend.' He looked at the litter of papers spread out on the desk. 'Damn!' he exclaimed. 'Just as everything was getting knocked into shape!' He banged his desk with his fist, then gave Maria a shamefaced look. 'Sorry, my dear. Temper!'

She smiled. 'Don't worry. These are minor details, honestly. If you've got to go, there's no question about it. Brand and I will work on it.'

And that was just what they did, for several hours more, to be interrupted by Charles' ring to announce his safe arrival in Inverness.

At ten o'clock the telephone rang again, and Maria, engrossed in writing, heard Brand leave to answer it. They had worked hard, paused only for coffee, and things were looking good. The atmosphere was pleasant and civilised, and she had scarcely given a thought to the fact that they were alone in the house.

That all changed a moment later when Brand returned and stood in the doorway. 'You're wanted on the phone,' he said, and she could almost see the icicles forming round his words. She looked up, puzzled both by his words and by the way they were said.

'Who is it?'

'Cassie. I told her you were busy, and she began to give me a message—and then I told her it might be better if *you* spoke to her.' No doubt about it, the temperature had dropped.

Maria picked up the telephone in the drawing room, and said: 'Hello, Cassie?'

'Sorry to phone, but Julian just rang me, frantic because he's lost his *fearfully* expensive watch, and he said he'd been trying to get you only you weren't in——'

'Yes. But what makes him think I might know?' asked an even more puzzled Maria.

'He thought he might have left it in your bedroom.'

'Ah!' Light dawned, and with it, understanding of why Brand's attitude might suddenly have changed.

'Cassie, did you tell Brand he'd been in to fix that loose door on my wardrobe?' Maria asked.

'Didn't get the chance, my love! He just said: "It might be better to speak to Maria," and went.'

'I *see*. Yes, he did take his watch off, but I saw him put it on again afterwards. If I remember rightly, he was going on to see his mother to mend her television. Tell him that, will you? He could have left it there.'

'I will. Hey, everything all right?'

'Everything's super.' Or was, Maria added under her breath. 'Must go, love, the advertising job's coming along nicely. I'll tell you all at the weekend.'

'Fine.' There was the noise of music in the background, a general hum of voices, and a clatter. It wasn't too difficult to assume that Cassie was entertaining. ' 'Bye for now.'

' 'Bye.' Maria hung up, very thoughtful for now. So Brand assumed that a man had left his watch in her bedroom—and he was apparently none too pleased. Why should that be?

Slightly less puzzled, beginning to feel quite amused and intrigued, she decided to go and make coffee before returning to work.

She was searching for cups when Brand said, from behind her: 'Well, well, and did you sort out your friend's little problem?'

'I did my best.' She had her back to him, and didn't turn round.

'Did he take it off so that he could check what time he had to leave?'

'No,' she said calmly, turning to face him. 'He took it off so that he wouldn't damage it when he mended my wardrobe door.'

'An original line. I must try it some time.' He smiled, and she didn't like the smile. 'I should have thought a *bed* was more in your line, not a wardrobe. Still, it takes all sorts.'

His face was hard, his eyes contemptuous. She suddenly thought with shock, My God, he's jealous! She began to laugh, the laughter pealing out, and she had to lean on the sink because it gave her a pain in her side, and she was helpless. Brand—jealous? Not possible, she would have thought, but there was no mistaking the expression on his face.

It made her say something she would not normally have dreamed of. 'Oh, I like a bit of variety occasionally,' she retorted. 'Don't *you*?' She laughed again. 'No, of course you don't—as I well remember!'

'You little tramp!' he spat out, and that did it. Enough was enough. The icy contempt in his face, the twisted mouth—she slapped him hard, wiping the expression from him. 'Don't you ever dare speak to me like that again!' she hissed. 'Ever. I've put up with a lot from you in these past weeks, one way or another. A *lot*. But I will not be called a tramp by *you* or anyone else. He went into my bedroom and he fixed a broken door—and then he left. Which is more than I could say of you. You wouldn't miss a trick, would you? Any opportunity, you're there——'

'I wasn't aware that I'd raped you,' he cut in, voice harsh and hard. 'It takes two, you know—and by God, you were asking——'

She struck out blindly at him, and he caught her wrist and held it so tightly she thought he would snap the bone. She cried out and he let it go, flinging her arm from him. She clutched her wrist, eyes wide with fear and Brand turned sharply on his heel and stalked out, slamming the door behind him. Maria rushed after him, caught up with him at the foot of the stairs and shouted: 'There's a lock on my bedroom door. I shall use it tonight, and every night I'm here. Are you listening? You—swine!'

He had paused, then without turning, he went on up the stairs. Trembling, Maria held on to the newel post. Bitterness welled up inside her. He had called her a tramp—and he had meant it. Then he had said something so unforgivable that it didn't bear thinking about. That finished everything. She wasn't staying here any longer, and when she got to London she was going to write in to Mike and tell him that this time she was leaving for good.

# CHAPTER TWELVE

MARIA sat on the bus and looked out of the window at the bleak windswept countryside. Her case was on the seat beside her, and she was on the way to the village to collect her car from the garage. It was mid-afternoon on a grey November Monday, and the weather matched her mood.

She had tried to telephone the station after the blazing row with Brand the previous night, but there had been no reply. She had decided to leave first thing the following morning, and once having decided, set to work calmly and coolly to finish her notes and drawings and leave them in order for Charles when he returned. She wrote him a letter explaining that she was leaving but would contact him. She gave no further reason; her emotions were too raw and jagged for any explanations.

She had wakened at six that morning, packed and tidied her room and gone downstairs, creeping very quietly so as not to wake Brand. She had telephoned the station several times, keeping the drawing room door tightly closed, and with no success.

It was on her sixth attempt, as she had leafed through a magazine and seen a picture of a car, that she remembered her own Mini, and realised that she could go north and collect it today. Why not? She had enough money with her—or at least her cheque book and bank card—and it would save a longer journey later. She searched through her handbag for the garage's letter, found it, and praying that it wasn't too early, phoned them. No reply again. 'Damn, oh, damn,' she muttered. She wrote the number on a piece of paper and put the letter back in her bag. It was only seven. After a quick breakfast she would phone again.

She carried out the telephone directory to the kitchen and while the kettle boiled, looked for a taxi number. She found one, used the kitchen extension to call, booked one for twenty minutes later, and made her coffee. She would go to the station, find out about trains there, have breakfast, call the garage to see if there was a bus service from anywhere, and take it from there.

Which was what she had done. There was a bus from Stirling, the garage man had assured her, but it ran only twice a day—she would get it, she knew that. Thanking him, she told him she would be in to collect her car later, then went to find a train to Stirling.

Now, hours later, she was nearly there. She lay back and shut her eyes. Brand would of course have discovered her absence by now, and possibly read the letter to Charles. She hadn't left him so much as a note, because she had absolutely nothing to say to him. Not any more, ever.

Her car was waiting, bright and clean and looking like new. She paid the owner and thanked him, then, on sudden impulse, walked to the grocery shop next door and bought a packet of biscuits and a carton of milk. She knew where she was going, she had known ever since she set out.

She was going on a last visit to the cottage. The key she had forgotten to return to Brand—and he probably wouldn't have accepted it—was still in her bag.

She drove slowly away, the engine purred, sweet and clean, and she was neither happy nor sad. She felt blank inside. She might feel pain when she entered the place that had filled her dreams, or she might feel nothing.

The water was lapping at the causeway, but she had known, with a sure inner instinct, that she would be in time. She drove carefully across; the trees were bare with the approach of winter, and it was a bleak lonely place, but when she left it tomorrow she would be free.

She left her car at the front and walked towards the door. No smoke came from the chimney this time, because it was empty. Brand, if he thought at all about her, would assume she was in London.

She opened the door and walked in, and Brand said: 'Hello, Maria. Now you're here, I can light the fire.' He was standing by it, and he bent and put a match to the laid wood and coal, and it flared up immediately. Maria wordless, clutching her heart, could only stand and watch.

He walked over to her. 'History repeats itself, doesn't it?' he said gently. 'Only this time—no fighting—no arguing. This time, love, it's different.'

'How—how——' she gasped.

'You left the number of the garage by the phone. I knew where you were going. I took a gamble that you'd come here for a last look, because I remembered what you said the other night.' He took her in his arms, and she was unresisting, still too shocked to do anything. 'I'd have looked a fool if you'd gone straight to London, wouldn't I? I'd have been stuck here alone.'

He drew her towards the fire, pushed her gently on to the settee, and sat beside her. 'I drove up here, I even hid my car so that you wouldn't see it and suspect. I had to wait for the tide to go out, and I'd checked your time, I knew you'd arrive when you did. I've been waiting an hour nearly, and I love you very much, and when I said those unforgivable things last night it was because I'd experienced jealousy for the first time in my life.'

'Love? You—you said you didn't know——'

'I didn't know it existed. Until I said goodbye to you outside your flat, and a light went out of my life. Why do you think I persuaded Mike to make you stay? It wasn't for your talent—although you've proved that—it was because I wanted you in my life. I'm patient, and I was prepared to wait. I wasn't prepared for what happened last night. Do you forgive me?'

Maria nodded. 'Oh, Brand love, why do you think *I* wanted to escape? It was because of my own feelings, feelings that began here weeks ago.' She looked down at the hand that held hers very firmly. 'You've scarcely been out of my thoughts or dreams since then——' She paused. 'It was why I had to come here, to exorcise the ghosts, if you like. Only I found you instead, and that's much better.'

He kissed her, a long, deep kiss that left no doubt, if doubt could still have existed, of his feelings for her. Huskily he said:

'How soon can we get married?'

'As soon as you like,' she whispered. The fire burned bright and true, and it was just as she had remembered.

'Then next week, by special licence,' he murmured, tracing a finger down her face to her neck. 'Do you want the good news or the bad news?'

'Oh! The bad news first,' she answered.

'The bad news,' he declared solemnly, 'is that we're stranded here until tomorrow.'

'Heavens!' she gasped, as her heartbeats quickened. 'And what's the good news?'

'The good news is——' he went to whisper in her ear, 'that there's only one bed, and—I have to confess, I can't sleep on the settee.'

'That's a shame,' she murmured. 'But I'm sure we can discuss the problem later.'

She was silenced as his mouth came down on hers. 'I think I'd like to discuss it now,' he whispered huskily after some minutes. 'Perhaps if we went up and—er—sized up the situation——'

'Mmm, sounds sensible!' she agreed as he pulled her to her feet. 'It sounds *very* sensible.'

Brand picked her up in his arms and held her closely to him. The next words he whispered were very private . . .

While many Harlequin authors say that writing was always in their blood, Mary Wibberley claims that as a child the idea of being a writer never even entered her head. For her, the future always meant becoming an artist, or perhaps a Wimbledon tennis champion!

But after marriage and the birth of her daughter, Mary thought she'd give writing a try. So she crept downstairs one night and began covering pages of paper with notes.

Her first novel did not meet with success, nor did her second, third, fourth, fifth, sixth or seventh. But to her surprise and delight, her eighth attempt, *The Black Niall* (Romance #1717), was accepted and published in 1973.

Mary Wibberley likes her heroines—and her heroes—to have a sense of humor. And no matter how hard she plans her characters, she finds that they take on personalities of their own. In fact, as she sits down in the morning to work, Mary will often wonder, "What on earth is going to happen today?"

# Harlequin Presents...

## Take these
## 4 best-selling novels
## FREE

That's right! FOUR first-rate Harlequin romance novels by four world renowned authors, FREE, as your introduction to the Harlequin Presents Subscription Plan. Be swept along by these FOUR exciting, poignant and sophisticated novels . . . . Travel to the Mediterranean island of Cyprus in **Anne Hampson**'s "Gates of Steel" . . . to Portugal for **Anne Mather**'s "Sweet Revenge" . . . to France and **Violet Winspear**'s "Devil in a Silver Room" . . . and the sprawling state of Texas for **Janet Dalley**'s "No Quarter Asked."

Join the millions of avid Harlequin readers all over the world who delight in the magic of a really exciting novel. SIX great NEW titles published EACH MONTH! Each month you will get to know exciting, interesting, true-to-life people . . . . You'll be swept to distant lands you've dreamed of visiting . . . . Intrigue, adventure, romance, and the destiny of many lives will thrill you through each Harlequin Presents novel.

  *The very finest
in romantic fiction*

*Get all the latest books before they're sold out!*

As a Harlequin subscriber you actually receive your
personal copies of the latest Presents novels immediately
after they come off the press, so you're sure of getting all
6 each month.

*Cancel your subscription whenever you wish!*

You don't have to buy any minimum number of books.
Whenever you decide to stop your subscription just let us
know and we'll cancel all further shipments.